GODDESS
Game

By

Sheila Lee Brown

Copyright 2025 by Sheila Lee Brown

All rights reserved. No part of this book may be reproduced in any form whatsoever, by photography, or xerography or by any other means, by broadcast or transmission, by translation into any kind of language, nor by recording electronically or otherwise, without the permission in writing from the author, except to quote brief passages in critical articles, reviews, or academic works.

This book is a work of fiction. Any resemblance to real persons, living or dead, is purely coincidental.

ISBN-978-1-946651-18-1

Published by TZ Books
www.tz-books.com

Chapter One:

"I need to get there!"

Thirty-eight-year-old Bethany stood in front of the corn chips in the snack aisle at the Village Pantry, struggling with the always tough decision of mild versus medium salsa. The annoyed voice startled her. She then felt a jolt as her cart, which was positioned to her side, jerked towards her. She had a hand resting on the handle and could stop it before impact.

Bethany turned to see an older woman riding one of the motorized carts. Bethany frowned but gave the lady the benefit of doubt, thinking that maybe the device wasn't easy to maneuver and it had been an accident. She was proven wrong when the woman grimaced and lurched forward again, jarring her cart once more.

"I don't have all day," the woman shrieked. "Move it or be moved!"

Bethany gripped the handle of her cart as if she were dangling over a cliff-side. Letting go would be perilous. Her chest tightened with the familiar mix of panic and frustration that came with these situations.

I'm in control, she told herself.

She felt a mix of emotions rolling through her body as every muscle tightened, readying for confrontation. It seemed lately that it was harder and harder to avoid these inconvenient interactions, despite her best efforts.

Here she was, shopping on a Monday afternoon, hoping to avoid the rush of after-work shoppers or those that shopped on the weekend. Having her groceries delivered was becoming more and more appealing. If only she could trust the shoppers to not just grab a random avocado off the pile without checking it for ripeness! She didn't.

I'm in control, she repeated to herself.

She wasn't sure how much she believed that, but the thought had a calming effect. Every time she had an unplanned interaction like this, she felt an unexplainable, wild fear and an anger at having her peace disturbed.

Bethany forced herself to take a deep, calculated breath. It gave her just enough distance from her emotions to do what she needed to do. The next action was as natural as exhaling.

Bethany allowed her gaze to shift slightly out of focus, backing out of the moment and into what she called the "safe room" in her mind. The fear and anger didn't touch her here. She paused to enjoy the peace of escaping the "real world."

Her safe room was a small, empty square room—like a bedroom, but without doors or windows. The walls and floor were white, though the ceiling was as dark as a night sky.

On the wall she was facing, several images appeared. It reminded Bethany of video options in an online search. And that was sort of what they were—snippets of potential futures that were based on her next actions. She could see the first few seconds of each one—there were probably a dozen—and she gave them a quick once over to see if any stood out.

Time stood still in this place and while she didn't need to decide quickly, she wanted to get out of the situation and move on with her life. Bethany had never tested out how long she could stay there, and sometimes she considered that if she grew too overwhelmed with life, she could just step out indefinitely. That would be trippy. After a few hundred years in the safe room, would she even remember what she was stepping back into?

Today wasn't the day to find out. Bethany was looking forward to a chill night of binge-watching. That seemed more entertaining than sitting in her mental safe space.

The videos populating the wall organized themselves. Bethany thought of this part as a filter for "most relevant." She began looking over the top ten.

The first three videos were a hard pass, though in her current mood they were somewhat appealing. In one, she took all the items out of the woman's basket and put it on the top shelf and walked away. It was such a wrong thing to do, truly mean, but Bethany let herself watch it longer than she should. It ended up in a confrontation with three more customers who saw what Bethany did and wanted her to apologize to the lady. So, a nope on that one.

In another, Bethany moved out of the way, but then followed the woman around the store, ramming into her motorized cart every time she stopped. This choice led to a confrontation with the store manager and being banned from the store. Again, another no.

One looked like a heated verbal assault. Bethany skipped right over it without even listening in. Even though the woman could be nicer, Bethany didn't want to get any further entangled with her than she was currently. She needed the path of least resistance, at least for the next ten to fifteen minutes, and she finally saw it. She sighed to herself. It was an obvious response, of course, but not satisfying in the least.

"I'm sorry," Bethany said with a smile that she hoped was convincing. "It's all yours. And might I say that is a lovely sweater you're wearing?"

Bethany did her best to sound authentic, though the sweater looked like a dog had eaten it, threw it up, and the woman had decided to wear it as a reflection of her personality.

Just as she witnessed in her safe room video, the compliment confused the woman and gave Bethany enough time to pull her cart backwards, turn it around and bolt in the opposite direction, still strangling the cart handle with her grip. No salsa today. She'd have to settle for eating plain corn chips.

At least she shouldn't have to worry about engaging with the woman again. That outcome didn't leave any residue of anger for the woman to want to act on. Bethany still had hers, though. One downside to using the safe room to avoid uncomfortable situations was that Bethany had to repress a lot of annoyance and anger to act her way out of the situation. She usually went home and burned it off with some intense yoga or other exercise. These days, she was in fantastic shape for being nearly forty years old.

More and more often, she was removing herself as quickly as she could. She didn't have the patience or interest in seeing if there was anything more for her to gain from the situation. Playing the shifting-reality game with strangers was more work than she was willing to put in. Bethany had her life worked out in a way that she was comfortable with. She would do a lot to maintain that. And had.

Bethany could easily come back to the store at another time. She glanced into her cart. She could make do with what she had already.

Emotionally, her equilibrium was disturbed, and she considered going for a run later to help clear her mind and rebalance herself. If she didn't, the imbalance might show up in her life as some other nuisance to work through.

Bethany pushed her cart and gritted her teeth. Yes, she chose to operate this way. And, yes, sometimes she wanted to scream. Instead, she followed the course of action laid out for her by her weird ability. That's how she stayed in control. But it was getting harder to cover up that it was an act.

Bethany took another deep breath in an effort to relax as she began making her way to the checkout. She stretched her neck by leaning her head side to side and shrugged her shoulders a few times, releasing them each time with an exhale. That helped a little.

As she rounded the end of the aisle and glanced down the next one, she saw the woman on the motorized cart had already moved on and was at the frozen meat section, arguing with a man there, presumably in her way. He didn't move and said something that left the old woman wide-eyed and mouth open. Bethany allowed herself a smile, but kept walking. Nothing good could come of that. She'd learned long ago that being a spectator to others' conflicts could pull you into their drama just as surely as being a participant.

Just before the checkout, Bethany noticed that one of the book displays was being dismantled and more greeting cards and "last-grab" items were being put out. Several of the books were marked as clearance items. Probably the result of the bookstore that had opened next door a few months ago. Her ex-husband, Caleb, owned and managed it, which still seemed odd to her as it was such a contrast to how he had operated when they were married. They actually got along really well, and she had promised to come by soon, though she kept finding reasons to delay.

Change begets change, she thought. She didn't like that fact, but you adjusted or you were adjusted. That had been her experience, even with her gift, and sometimes because she had used her gift to do just that.

A greeting card caught her eye, and she stopped and grabbed it off the rack. As an illustrator herself, she appreciated the work of other artists. This card had a cartoon cat on it with a word bubble saying, "It's whatever, Bishes!" She chuckled. The happy-go-lucky expression on the cat's face said it all. It did not care and was okay with that. If only.

Voices coming up behind Bethany jostled her into action, reminding her that she should head out. She put the card down and began moving towards the checkout. Her mind videos were useful but also held the potential for chaos. If she chose one and enacted it, she needed to follow it closely or strange, related things might show up later.

There was that time last month when she decided she was going to ad lib what she needed to say to an exterminator that stopped by the house. He was offering his services at a discount because he was treating the homes of two of the neighbors. In a rare moment, she had answered a knock at the door, thinking her housemate and friend, Jenna, had forgotten her keys again, and there he was.

Knowing she could just close the door at any moment, she tried to just say no, but he had thwarted nearly every polite way she was trying to tell him she wasn't interested. She finally went into her safe room and found a way out that didn't seem so rude and didn't leave any annoyance on his part, but just before she had completely acted it out, she remembered a pun she had seen somewhere and couldn't resist…

"Where do bugs get off a train?" Bethany had asked.

The man looked confused.

"At the *infest-station*?" Bethany answered with an expectant grin. "Is that where you get off, too?" She asked, already laughing. "For work?"

The man frowned, and that's when Bethany realized she had gone too far off script. She had gone back into her safe room and the only option she was willing to proceed with was closing the door and waiting for him to go away.

In the end, it was the result was what she wanted, but she could have done without him looking at her like she was mentally unstable. He would probably talk about her to the neighbors, and that could have its own repercussions for her later.

Not long after, she had a trail of ants in the kitchen and had to call an exterminator. She made sure it wasn't that guy, but she knew it was a penalty for not following the script.

Bethany had tested the boundaries of her safe room many times over the years and always regretted it. Still, she occasionally felt a little rebellious about it. The parameters of what she had to do seemed increasingly specific and limiting. A part of her wanted to revolt and let things go how they might. That seemed a little scary. The other part wanted a quiet life. That part had won out.

The safe room had been a part of Bethany's life since high school. God, the Universe - whatever you wanted to call it—had gifted her with these glimpses of the future right along with puberty. It seemed natural to use it to choose the paths that offered her the best life. Or at least the safest life. She wasn't a fan of taking risks, and, with her glimpses into the future, she didn't have to.

As Bethany pushed her cart, she watched for any evidence that she might have delayed her departure longer than she should have. She hurriedly maneuvered her way to the checkout, holding her breath as a cart passed by behind her as she stopped to assess where she should go. Even these small moments of uncertainty triggered what she felt was irrational anxiety.

Things were already showing up differently than what she had seen. Geez. She couldn't even stop to be amused by a greeting card without rippling the surface of her carefully maintained reality.

The lines at the self-checkout were long, so she pulled into one of the regular checkout lanes where there was only one cart ahead of her. A lady wrangled two toddlers as she attempted to put her groceries on the conveyor belt. The kids were trying to help, too, almost dropping each item that they picked up and tried to toss over to the moving conveyor.

Bethany smiled at the scene, watching as one kid picked up a bag of rice and lifted it. The rice shifted inside the plastic and folded over on itself, slipping out of his hands. His brother assisted the next attempt, and they lifted it together.

Bethany had illustrated several children's books, and the energy of kid-helpfulness would be something she might try to capture in a drawing. She reached out and grabbed the package of rice just as they had it balanced precariously over the cart edge and it was about to fall. The woman smiled a thank you and turned her attention to the cashier who was ringing up everything and the bag person who was asking if they could mix the meat with other products.

Bethany nodded an acknowledgement and then looked away quickly, remembering that she did not want to engage with anyone more than she had to. So far, so good. She was close to getting out unscathed. Just a few more minutes.

While Bethany stared an unnaturally long time at a box of sour blue raspberry gum, waiting her turn, she felt the nudge of a shopping cart from behind. She tensed, sure she was about to pay for not leaving as quickly as she could. She turned enough to see a man with a cart behind her. It was the same guy the woman in the motorized cart had pounced on after leaving Bethany. He apparently had survived. He was looking at something on the end cap and not paying attention. His cart had rolled forward and into her with no real force.

As she turned, the man glanced over and noticed his cart and pulled it back. Something about his presence made her pause, made her usual impulse to retreat switch off - at least for a few moments.

"Sorry," he said.

Bethany watched him for a moment, assessing. He seemed normal enough. Even attractive, with a nicely lined jaw. She watched him as he placed something back on the end-cap. When he looked back again, their eyes met. Bethany was struck by the intensity of the blueness of his eyes.

She opened her mouth, considering how to avoid any awkwardness, but before she could do or say anything, her mind slipped into the safe room without her triggering it.

Chaos erupted.

The videos appeared, but they began moving insanely fast, changing in such rapid succession that Bethany couldn't review them as she normally would. This was the first time she had not felt in control in her safe room, and it was a little unnerving. As her mind processed that, she found herself drawn into one particular future. Instead of watching, she began experiencing a series of scenes, like a highlight reel of her life with this man, popping into each one like an extra observer from within the version of herself living that life.

From making dinner together to working on a house project that she knew he would be surprised and happy about to hiking in the woods, the images were coming and going too fast for her to focus on any particular one. It occurred to her that they were all fairly mundane. They seemed to be ordinary life moments. And she noticed the matching wedding bands they wore. But more than the scenes themselves, it was the feelings that overwhelmed her - a sense of safety without constraint, of being truly seen and accepted, of joy in simple, shared moments.

"Husband," she whispered in his ear in a vision before kissing him lightly on the neck. The intimacy of it shook her - not just physical closeness, but the emotional vulnerability she'd spent years avoiding.

The images rolled on and Bethany felt something opening up within her, an emotion stronger than the anger she had been suppressing. She loved this man. Not only did she love him, she felt that there could be no one more amazing. If she had to judge from what she was seeing, he felt the same about her. These weren't just visions of a possible future - they were glimpses of a life lived fully, one she had never conceived of as a possibility.

The visions ended as abruptly as they started. Bethany's consciousness was back in the Village Pantry. She was in the checkout line, and she was gaping at the man who, apparently, would one day be her husband.

Chapter Two

Bethany gulped as she processed the situation. She tried to calm her racing heart, to slip back into her usual controlled state, but something had shifted. For the first time in decades, she felt truly present in the moment, truly alive - and it was terrifying and exhilarating all at once.

Here she stood with an opportunity most people would never have. She was in the presence of the man who would be her husband. She knew it without a doubt. The visions still echoed in her mind, tantalizing glimpses of a happiness she hadn't even known she was missing.

That is, if she followed the right path. Panic set in. She hadn't seen what she needed to do in this moment to set her in the right direction. She tried to tap into her gift again, but for the first time since it had appeared in her life, it didn't respond. It was like reaching for a handrail that should be there and finding only empty air.

She was staring and she suspected she was coming off as some sort of weirdo. She managed a small smile as she tried to figure out what to do. Her palms were sweating on the shopping cart handle. How did normal people do this? How did they just ... talk to each other without knowing the outcome?

Bethany could still feel all the emotions she had for this man as the visions winked out. But at this time and place, he was a stranger. The disconnect between what she knew of their future and the reality of this moment made her feel slightly dizzy.

Bethany grounded herself in the moment and realized that she hadn't responded to his apology. She felt like she needed to say the perfect thing. How often did a person come across their future love and know it? There had to be a reason her gift had shown her this now, but, without it working, she felt like a teenager again, awkward and unsure.

She let her gaze slip out of focus, attempting to tap into her gift again, but it still wasn't working. Bethany knew she couldn't just let this opportunity slip away. She felt like a lot was riding on what she said in the next few moments, and she had no gift-guided script to follow.

Bethany looked down at his groceries and saw beef jerky and pretzels, a 6-pack of canned soda, and several other boxes and bags of snack foods. They might end up making their dinners together at some point, but currently it appeared that he liked to eat junk. Bethany frowned, unable to hide her disapproval. In her vision, they'd cooked healthy meals together. This didn't fit the narrative she'd seen.

"I said I was sorry," the man said. "No need to take it out on the food."

"What?" Bethany said. "I didn't mean…," she began, but she couldn't think of anything to say to neutralize the situation. Her mind raced through possibilities, but without her gift to show her the outcomes, she was flying blind. Everything she thought to say seemed wrong.

"What have you got in your cart? Oh my," the man said, glancing past Bethany to her cart. Even the corn chips she bought were organic. "You're one of those people who thinks they eat better than everyone else, right?"

"Not…," she was about to say "not really", but the truth was she did. She wasn't perfect by any means, but keeping her energy high, her mind clear, and her body in motion were important to her. The words stuck in her throat as she realized how judgmental she must seem. This was exactly why she needed her gift - to keep her from alienating people before she even got to know them.

"I can help who's next," the teenage cashier said while looking pointedly at Bethany. The woman with the two kids was moving towards the exit and Bethany hadn't put any of her food on the conveyor. She felt herself flushing under the combined attention.

Not knowing what to say, Bethany turned and began unloading her food. She didn't have much, so she grabbed a divider and put it at the end. Her hands were shaking slightly, and she nearly dropped a bunch of bananas.

"Yep. Let's make sure your good, quality food doesn't touch my atrocious processed gunk," the man said as he began sliding his food onto the conveyor. He sounded a bit snarky, but he was also smirking, as if he was enjoying prodding her. Could that be his way of flirting? Weird. The visions had shown them connecting easily. Why was this so hard?

"Listen, I don't care what you eat," Bethany said. It seemed the safest thing to say, though she regretted how defensive it sounded. "But I don't want to pay for your groceries."

The man snorted and continued loading his items onto the belt. The beeps from the register let Bethany know the cashier was quickly scanning her items, only slowed by having to input the codes for the fresh produce. Each beep felt like a countdown to her chances slipping away.

"Are you always so defensive about your food?" Bethany asked, feeling a little emboldened by the prospect of their future union. She noted that what he had were snack-type things and not any staples for meals. He didn't look like someone who ate like that regularly, but she didn't want to make any other presumptions.

"Not really," the man sighed. "I don't mean to be a jerk. It's been a day. I barely survived some old lady trying to bulldoze me with one of those electric carts."

"Ah. Yeah. She got me, too," Bethany said, feeling a spark of connection. Finally, common ground!

"I guess no one is safe," the man gave a small smile. "Based on her attitude, I imagine she's having an even worse day." He finished putting his items on the belt. "Oh, well. What doesn't kill you makes you stronger, right?"

"Or it maims you for life," Bethany laughed, then cringed. "I was joking. It wasn't as funny out loud as it was in my head."

The man chuckled. Bethany wasn't sure how to take it. Was he laughing with her or at her?

"We're ready to take payment," the cashier said.

Bethany turned to the cashier. As she made payment, she desperately tried to access her gift again. The moment was slipping away, and she had no idea how to hold on to it.

"Hope the rest of your day gets better," she finally said as she turned to leave. The words felt inadequate and wrong. This surely wasn't how their first meeting was supposed to go.

"Thanks," the man said and turned his attention to the cashier.

Outside, it was a nice cool afternoon with the warmth of the sun still beaming overhead. Bethany walked over to the bike stand just outside the store and took her time placing her bags into the cart attached to her bike while she side-eyed the grocery store exit, waiting for (what should she call him? Dream Guy?) to come out. Her heart was still racing from their interaction, and she felt slightly nauseated from anxiety.

A whiff of coffee drew her attention to the bookstore just down the frontage of the strip mall. She had created the logo and font for the store name: "Bookmarked"

It looked even better on the storefront than he had on her computer. This was no time to get distracted, though.

Bethany glanced back over at the grocery store doors. Dream Guy was going to walk through any second. What was her plan?

She attempted to enter her safe room, and it still wasn't happening. How did normal people do this? She thought through some of the dates she had been on over the past four years since the divorce. The only thing she had learned was how to extricate herself from situations she didn't want to be in.

Seriously, though. She needed some sort of reason to approach Dream Guy. If she didn't have her gift, she would just have to use her imagination.

One option: She could start riding her bike towards him as he came out and hope for an encounter. What would she say? And what if he walked out too slowly and it became obvious she was trying to wait on him? She imagined herself awkwardly circling the parking lot on her bike like some sort of creeper.

This plan needed more stealth.

Another option: She could take the lead and start walking back in as if she forgot something. But she didn't really want to leave her groceries unguarded, and what would she even say?

That was the crux of the issue. She had nothing she could say to him that wouldn't come across as bizarre or strange.

For instance, "Hey stranger, I think we'd make a sweet couple. Let's go out and build a life together!" might be over the top.

People walking in and out were glancing over at her. She realized she must look odd standing there next to her bike, making faces as she imagined out various scenarios. Thinking through possible futures in your mind wasn't timeless. They also weren't a sure thing. He should be out soon, though, so she didn't want to leave. She left her bike and walked over to peek inside the bookstore.

Caleb had done a great job of making it look inviting. The front, right corner was a small coffee shop. It had several small tables and comfy chairs. Bethany had put together many of the displays that were out. Caleb and his new staff had done the rest. She could imagine herself sitting there and enjoying a book and a coffee—ideally if there were no other people.

Bethany knew from helping out that Caleb made sure the children's section had all the books she had illustrated over the years. He had always been pretty good about supporting her. She leaned towards the glass, trying to see further in and happened to focus on her reflection and grimaced. She was wearing her old, ratty college sweatshirt and a pair of yoga pants. Working from home had its benefits and after doing it for a while, she rarely thought about how it translated to real world interactions.

Bethany felt eyes on her and saw that inside the bookstore, Caleb had noticed she was standing there and was making his way towards the door. Her anxiety ratcheted up another notch.

For the second time that day, Bethany froze. She wasn't sure she wanted to be seen with Caleb. Something just felt wrong about having her ex-husband and future husband in the same place before her future husband even knew he was her future husband.

Besides, she and Caleb got along so well, most people thought they were together. And when they found they weren't, she was sure they wondered why. But they hadn't been together like that in years. She couldn't risk Dream Guy assuming that they were and ruining everything!

Bethany saw the movement of the grocery store door open and instinctively turned to see, of course, Dream Guy stepping outside. Caleb would pop out of the bookstore at any moment. She could see no way to make this situation work. To make matters even worse, her cell phone began to ring.

Bethany pulled the phone from her back pocket and saw that it was her housemate, friend, and business partner, Jenna.

"Hey, what's going on?" Bethany answered, turning from Caleb and Dream Guy. She did glance over at Dream Guy for a moment, watching him walk down a row of cars in the parking lot. Each step felt like a step away from their future life together.

"I'm at the ER," Jenna said. She sounded strained, but her naturally bubbly personality was there, too. "I have to have emergency surgery."

"What?" Bethany asked. She was no longer thinking about Caleb or Dream Guy. She turned her full attention to Jenna. "What happened? Are you okay?"

"I'm fine. Well, I'll be fine. My mom is here," Jenna said. There was a long pause. "I have a huge favor to ask."

"Why are you having emergency surgery?" Bethany asked. "That sounds serious."

"It's no big deal," Jenna said. "I had some pain in my lower abdomen when I was dropping off books. It's happened before, so I wasn't worried at first. But it got pretty bad, and I went to urgent care. Turns out I have an inguinal hernia, and it's not ideal, but I have to have surgery. In the next couple of hours, to be exact. I shouldn't have to stay in the hospital more than overnight, but…"

"But…?" Bethany prompted. She noticed several cars leaving the parking lot. Dream guy was probably in one. She'd have to figure that out later. Jenna needed her to be present.

"That's where the favor comes in," Jenna said. "I'll need you to take care of Rufus for me for a few days."

Bethany made a fist and mouthed "No", but didn't say it. Rufus was Jenna's dog and while Bethany didn't have a problem with Rufus, she didn't like taking care of animals. Bethany tried to tap into her ability again, but got nothing. *Crap!*

"I know how you feel about animals and I'm sorry to ask. I'll owe you big time," Jenna offered.

"I thought you would only be staying overnight," Bethany said, immediately feeling a little like a jerk.

"I'm going to my mom's house when I get out so she can help me. She's allergic to dogs, so I can't take him to her house. The surgery is laparoscopic. I should recover quickly. My mom's got a recliner that would be easier for me to get in and out of than anything we have at the house."

Bethany saw Caleb standing at the bookstore door, watching her. He gave a slight wave to show he would wait. She nodded in acknowledgement. Bethany was committed to talking to him now. With no other actual choices, she resolved herself to the fact that the day was going to go how the day was going to go.

Tonight was shaping up to be a binge-watching evening. She needed some high-quality distraction. She would even settle for low-quality distraction. At least Rufus was a decent couch buddy.

Even without her gift, she knew helping was the right thing to do, even if she didn't want to. She owed Jenna a lot. In this case, she could at least feel good about helping a friend.

"Of course I'll do it," Bethany said, attempting to smile and force that energy into her words. "I think I know his routine well enough." Bethany wondered if this situation resulted from not getting out of the store more quickly. Of course, she wouldn't have encountered her future husband. The thought of Dream Guy made her stomach clench again. How was she supposed to find him again?

Jenna let out a sigh of relief, reminding Bethany that she was still engaged in conversation.

"Thank you so much," Jenna said. "I sent you a couple of work items. Nothing too extreme, but time sensitive. My mom will pick up my laptop tomorrow so I can work if I'm able. I'll do my best to keep you updated."

"Take care," Bethany said. "I hope everything goes well. Tell your mom to text me when you're out of surgery to let me know how things went."

"I will."

Silence. Bethany realized that if she was about to go into surgery, she might feel a little uneasy.

"Are you nervous?" Bethany asked, forcing herself to focus on her friend rather than her own troubles.

"A little," Jenna said. "You know me. I'm adaptable. I'll get through it. No problem." A brief pause and low voices. "They are here to put me under. I've gotta go."

Bethany thought Jenna's positivity sounded a little aloof. She wondered if that was how she sounded when she faked her way through things. Without her safe room, she wasn't sure what else to say, and the conversation was over, anyway.

"Talk to you soon."

"Bye, Beth," Jenna said.

"Bye."

Bethany slid her phone back into her pocket and turned to see Caleb exiting the bookstore. She caught a whiff of dark coffee mixed with new book smell. It was lovely.

"Hi," he said. "I saw you lingering. I thought you might be here to see the store."

Jumping into a casual conversation felt surreal after everything that had just happened. In the last fifteen minutes, she'd met her future husband, completely failed to connect with him, lost her supernatural gift, and agreed to dog-sit while her best friend had surgery.

For Caleb, this was just another day. Her mind was spinning with possibilities and regrets about Dream Guy. Maybe she could ask around about him? But how would she explain knowing they were meant to be together? Even in her head, it sounded crazy.

"Are you all right?" Caleb asked when she didn't respond right away.

"Uh, yeah, I guess," Bethany said, rubbing her forehead to soothe a headache forming. "I just found out that Jenna is having emergency surgery, so I have to take care of Rufus."

She didn't bother telling him about the dream guy. For one, awkward. Second, Caleb didn't know about her gift even though they had been together nearly thirteen years and married nine of those before it ended.

"Emergency surgery?" Caleb took a couple of steps toward Bethany. "She okay?"

"She seems to think she'll be fine. Rufus, on the other hand, needs someone to feed him and let him out to do his evening potty time."

"Of course," Caleb said. "Do you need me to help with anything?"

"I think I'm okay," she said. In her head, she knew she was not okay, but she was ready to hide away at home and ponder her next moves. She pointed to her bike and the grocery bags. "I also need to get these home."

"Another time, then," he said. "Give Rufus a pat on the head for me."

"Will do," Bethany smiled. She and Caleb had been good friends even before they dated and then got married. The uncomfortable part was that she had initiated the divorce. Even after four years of not being together, she wasn't sure that he understood why. She had used her gift to maneuver out of every unpleasant conversation while still maintaining the friendship. "See ya."

He waved goodbye and went back inside the bookstore. Bethany sighed and began her bike ride home. She lived close enough that as long as it wasn't raining, it was nice to bike over for shopping. If she had lots of time and didn't need to carry much, she would walk.

She followed the sidewalk up several blocks and then up the driveway to the house she had grown up in. It became hers when her mom passed away. Bethany didn't have any other close family. She felt lucky to have a friend like Jenna that felt like family.

Bethany left her bike in the garage and opened the door to make her way to the kitchen to put away her groceries. Rufus bounded in, wagging his tail and happy to see her. He was a rescue dog and a mystery mix of breeds. He looked like a medium-sized labrador-beagle mix with dark fur and a playful personality.

"Looks like the two of us are hanging out tonight," Bethany said as she gave Rufus a couple of scratches behind his ear.

He wagged his tail happily and then burp-vomited right at her feet.

Chapter Three

Bethany snuggled under the covers in bed. She could hear Rufus pattering around the house, looking for Jenna. His nails clicked rhythmically against the hardwood floors as he went from room to room. She was grateful there had been no more vomit. She had cleaned it up, dry heaving several times.

The evening was leveling out. She had a text that the surgery had gone well and Jenna was resting. Hopefully, Rufus would settle down for the night soon, too. He had a dog bed in nearly every room and plenty of options.

Bethany had forced herself to go for a quick run before dinner to help clear her mind. After a shower, she had dinner on the couch with Rufus while streaming some shows that required little thought. She couldn't focus on what she was watching, though, and mainly stayed there because Rufus fell asleep with his head on her leg. Her mind kept drifting back to the grocery store, replaying and analyzing every moment with Dream Guy.

Bethany pulled the blanket up to her chin and then over her face.

It was all so embarrassing!

She shifted, cocooning herself further.

Bethany wished she could talk to Jenna. She even considered calling Caleb, but she didn't want to lean on that friendship too much. She didn't have many people in her life that she could confide in. That had been a choice, she realized now. It was easier to avoid deep connections when you were always calculating the safest path through every interaction.

Deep connections could also hurt. Her father had been in an accident when she was young—before she even had her gift. She lost her mom just before she and Caleb had gotten divorced. That was probably the worst year of her life. She had navigated it all as best she could. She had the house and was able to shift her life there fairly easily. But her gift had shown her the way through everything. Why would it have been any different?

Bethany was especially glad she had the house. It helped her feel close to her parents, even though they were gone. She had given Jenna the larger room with the master bathroom. Bethany used the other two bedrooms, one for her bedroom and one for her work area. The arrangement seemed appropriate. In a lot of ways, especially in their partnership, Bethany felt like a kid and Jenna felt like the parent.

Bethany took three deep breaths. The blanket held the warmth of her breath. She couldn't activate her safe room, but the breaths and the warmth were soothing.

She let herself think about the day in a more focused way. It had started out as a normal Monday. She worked the first half of the day clearing her bookkeeping client duties. She would have spent the early afternoon illustrating if she had any current work. Jenna brought in that side of her income. That opening in her schedule had given her the time to go to the grocery store.

Her breathing slowed as she sank deeper into the memory. Nothing odd happened until she encountered Dream Guy, or at least not until she encountered him up close. She had noticed him talking to the motorized cart lady moments before. You'd think there would be a lightning flash or special feeling when she first saw him. There hadn't been, though.

If she hadn't run into that lady, she probably would have still been shopping when he was leaving. And she saw he had run into that lady. Could the lady be the root of all the problems? The Universe worked in mysterious ways sometimes.

None of it was making much sense. Bethany almost felt like she did when she first discovered her gift and also discovered that other people didn't have something similar. Most people can imagine what will happen or speculate, but she had never met or heard of anyone who could foresee the outcome of social interactions like she could.

Unfortunately, that was the extent of her ability. She couldn't use it to win the lottery or make bets with any certainty. It seemed centered around being able to manage other people. Like a superpower designed specifically for introverts, she thought with a drowsy smile.

She had thought about her gift a lot over the years. After reading several books on energy, spirituality, and a bunch of other stuff that fell into what she categorized as "woo-woo", she had come to her own conclusions about it.

It seemed to Bethany that when she was in a social situation with someone or a group of people, her safe room tapped into the possibilities of the interactions created by their energies mingling. For most people, managing a person or a group might be an art form that they enjoyed. It might even be intimidating because that person wouldn't know how things would go.

However, Bethany always knew. That is, if she used her safe room. And she usually did because she didn't want to have to guess about things.

Sometimes she considered that she could easily manipulate herself into better jobs or opportunities by using her gift. She had found, though, that she was okay with a smaller, quieter life. The more you had, the more people wanted to interact with you, and it was a downward spiral from there.

That was one reason she was so grateful for Jenna. They had

known each other since grade school and were close friends. Jenna didn't mind interacting with people at all, even without a safe room. It made for a good partnership. Jenna helped to get Bethany illustrating work and took a cut of the income. Jenna also had other revenue streams. She was a real go-getter.

Jenna didn't even know about Bethany's gift or that Bethany had used it countless times to get her way with things. Bethany felt a little guilty about it, but she did try to make sure Jenna always benefited from the end result as well. As Bethany's consciousness drifted, she wondered if that justification was enough.

Bethany shifted again under the blanket. She didn't hear Rufus anymore. He must have curled up on one of his beds. Between the darkness of being in the blanket and the quiet of the house, Bethany had the surreal feeling of floating.

Her mind drifted closer to sleep. She yawned. Today brought unfamiliar territory. She needed to figure out why Dream Guy had caused her safe room to go away. The unknown made her nervous.

Thinking about Dream Guy caused her to drift back into the details of what she had seen with him. The feelings attached to the images still lingered and were what had made the biggest impression on her. Bethany cared for this man in a way that she had not cared for Caleb. She respected and admired him. She felt like she could be herself with no need for her gift with him and she was comfortable with him being himself.

As Bethany reflected on the visions, the joy she had experienced came flooding back. It felt as if she must be glowing like a lightbulb, but filled with gratefulness and love. She closed her eyes, savoring the feeling and wondering how she would find him and how she could make it all really happen. The warmth of possibility followed her down into sleep.

"You think you're so smart?"

It took Bethany a moment to realize that she had fallen asleep and was now dreaming.

Her dream body tensed. She was standing in front of her open high school locker, one of her drawings attached to the inside with a magnet—two cartoon cats punching each other. One was smiling happily while the other snarled angrily. She couldn't remember why she had drawn that.

The voice she had heard was familiar. It was Sandra Lunn, one of the meanest people Bethany had encountered during her teen years. They had once been friends in elementary school, but things had changed during junior high.

"I'm talking to you," Sandra said.

Bethany turned. The entire situation was familiar. It had actually happened. Sandra wasn't looking at Bethany, but at a girl three lockers down. Bethany thought her name was Lana. Lana was cowering as Sandra leaned into her face and pushed her against her locker.

"Next time you give the right answer in class," Sandra said. "I'm *going to find you after school and punch you in the face."* She punctuated the threat with a bang to the locker door that made Lana and Bethany flinch. The movement drew Sandra's attention to Bethany.

"You got something to say?" she asked.

Bethany looked at Lana and could see the plea for help in her eyes. She looked powerless and small next to Sandra, who somehow grew a foot taller than everyone else over the summer before high school. Sandra's anger was irrational, but she would do what she said, and who wanted to get punched in the face?

Bethany gulped and entered her safe room and selected her best option.

As she walked away, leaving Lana to fend for herself, she felt a small twinge of guilt that she quickly pushed out of sight. She was safe. She was okay. Lana could take care of herself. It wasn't her problem. As she turned the corner to go to her next class, the hallway disappeared, and she saw Lana standing there. Behind her were several paths, showing an adult Lana in different professions and family situations.

"I never gave the right answer in class after that," Lana said. She ran her hand through her hair and shrugged. *"I learned to be quiet."*

Bethany could see the more successful and happier life paths behind Lana begin crumbling away. All that was left was a frowning, nail-biting Lana, working in a cubicle amongst many.

She looked worn and tired.

Bethany took a step towards Lana, thinking she might try to explain. She had seen other options where she could help Lana, but it made Bethany's life harder and why should they both suffer?

Instead, Bethany found herself outside the high school cafeteria, talking to a young Jenna.

"Really, Jen," Bethany was saying.

"You're not making any sense," Jenna said. She was watching people coming out of the building as if she were looking for someone.

"I can see how something will play out. I can look over a bunch of options and then I get to choose the best one. And it works!"

"Does it work on math tests?" Jenna said with a grin. "We both can use some help with that."

"No," Bethany said with a sigh. "I think it's limited to social interactions."

"Beth, it sounds like you're using your imagination," Jenna said. She put her hand on Bethany's shoulder. "We all do that. It either keeps us from doing something or makes us want to do it. It's not magic."

"But," Bethany began. She had thought Jenna would be more open than that.

"Can you use it to get Sean to go out with me?" Jenna nudged Bethany and pointed out Sean walking out of the cafeteria with two of his friends.

"Maybe. It's not that cut and dry," Bethany said. *"I guess it just helps me stay out of trouble."*

"Sounds like boring magic," Jenna said.

"Yeah," Bethany said. *"I suppose it is."* She elbowed Jenna and laughed. *"I guess it's not such a great idea after all."*

"Idea?"

"I was just joking around, seeing how it sounded saying it out loud to someone. I was thinking of creating a character that had the power to see the future and choose what they want. Maybe I could make a comic or something?"

"No offense, but I don't think that story would be very interesting."

"Maybe not," Bethany smiled.

"Hey, let's go talk to Sean. He's with Caleb. Aren't you two in art class together?"

"Yeah, he kinda sucks at drawing," Bethany said with a laugh. *"But he's nice."*

The scene shifted to later that day in English class. She and Jenna had their desks pushed together, talking about the assignment they had been partnered up to complete. They needed to choose one of the books they had read for class that year and rewrite the ending and read the new ending to the class. Since many of the classics had formulaic endings, this was an opportunity to be creative and have fun.

"Do you have some ideas?" Jenna asked. "I thought this was English class. Isn't creative writing an elective?"

"I have a few ideas," Bethany said. "I don't mind the writing. I just don't want to read it in front of class."

"Hmmm...," Jenna said. "I don't want to write. You don't want to read. It just so happens that I don't mind getting up in front of the class. Seems like we may be able to create something here that works for both of us."

Bethany smiled and nodded in agreement. Just like she had seen herself do in the vision from her safe room. It was the first of many manipulations that would define their relationship going forward.

Her surroundings shifted again. Bethany had the tiniest awareness that she was being manipulated and pulled into particular memories and that she should be able to stop it if she wanted, but she drifted into the next scene and became part of the next interaction.

Art class. College.

"Those are so good!" the girl sitting next to Bethany leaned over their shared table, trying to better see what Bethany was sketching before class started. The room smelled of old paint and

canvas. "Oh, my gosh! Is that Professor Jarmon? That's definitely Clarissa, and Tyrone, and..."

Bethany closed her sketchbook. She always drew caricatures or cartoons of teachers and classmates in each class. More and more, she found she didn't want to engage with others. It seemed like a lot of effort went into trying not to stand out. Standing out was when the most chaos showed up. And when people decided to take you down a notch or two.

"Thanks," Bethany said. "They're kinda fun, but it's not what we're here to do."

They both glanced at the old sneaker at the front of the desk in between them. It looked like it had a hard life of running. Scuffed soles and discolored fabric told a story.

"I guess that's what we're drawing today," Bethany said.

"Your drawings are more fun," the girl said. "You should draw something for the literary journal. They publish a few art pieces each semester."

"The literary journal?"

"Yeah, the school literary journal. Haven't you seen the flyers?" The girl pointed to a flyer calling for submissions taped to the art room bulletin board.

Bethany had considered the idea. She even went as far as getting some drawings ready to submit. At the last minute, she tucked them back into her portfolio case and left them there. Another opportunity avoided, another potential connection severed *before it could form.*

As she looked up from her portfolio, she found she was in the whiteness of her safe room. The portfolio was gone. All four walls filled with dozens of squares of videos showing time after time she had used her gift to avoid something unpleasant or potentially embarrassing. The videos played simultaneously, a cacophony of missed chances. She spun round and round, overwhelmed by the number of scenes surrounding her and exposing what she could see as her cowardice.

She noticed she was also seeing the effects of her actions on the people she manipulated. Things that she never knew about. The scenes filled with hurt, grief, missed opportunities, and stagnation. The videos played like a highlight reel of her cowardice:

- *There was the time she saw her neighbor's dog getting loose and chose the path where she went inside instead of helping catch him. The dog was hit by a car. She could have prevented it, but she hadn't wanted to be late for a client meeting.*
- *The morning she saw her senior neighbor struggling with groceries and pretended she hadn't seen him. Later she learned he had fallen that day, though thankfully someone else had helped him.*
- *The community art fair where she might have made friends with other local artists, but she'd seen potential drama in one timeline and used it as an excuse to avoid the entire event.*

Around the squares of videos, she could still see the white of walls like a grid. The squares dropped away and the white grid that was left turned into silver bars. It was a cage, and Bethany was trapped inside.

Everything was now dark except for a light just outside the cage. Bethany walked over slowly. This dream had a different feel to it than any dream she had before. As she neared the wall of the cage closest to the light, she noticed it had a keyhole. It was the door, a way out. She looked down at what the light was shining on, and it was a key, lying on the dark floor outside the cage. If she just knelt down and stretched her arm out as far as she could, she just might...

Bethany knelt and as she reached for the key, it slid away from her. Bethany followed it with her gaze because even though it moved into the darkness, it had its own glow that illuminated it as it moved across the floor. It stopped at and highlighted a doorway that Bethany hadn't been able to see before. Bethany could see someone there, a female silhouette, standing just inside the frame. The shadow-woman bent down and picked up the key, tapping it in her hand like a disciplinarian's rod. But she didn't lift it enough so Bethany could see her face in its glow.

"My turn," the shadow woman said. Her voice hinted at amusement. She backed into the doorway and disappeared into darkness with the key.

"Let me out of here!" Bethany shouted, shaking the cage wall. She maintained a certain amount of lucidity and shouted again, "I know this isn't real! This is a dream!"

Before she could do anything further with that thought, she immediately had to cover her eyes as the darkness outside the cage flickered and the brightness of the sun nearly blinded her. When she could adjust her vision, she saw she was still in the cage, but now dangling over a vast expanse of water, an ocean that stretched out to the horizon. She looked up at the rocky edge above her. The cage was hanging from a rope attached to a metal rod extending from the side of the cliff several feet below the top.

As Bethany wondered how she could possibly get out of the cage and climb up to the top, a sound behind her caused her to turn around.

In the distance and moving towards her with terrifying speed, she could see a giant wave in the ocean. It rolled forward at an impossible size. Bethany's breath caught. No one could survive that. It looked like it could easily wash away entire cities. And it was coming straight for her!

Panic took over and Bethany shook the cage, trying to figure out how to get out. Then again, she wasn't sure where she could even go if she got out.

Bethany could smell the salt and feel the mist of water and hear the roar of the wave as it got closer and closer. She could feel absolute terror as she froze in place. She couldn't even manage a scream.

Bethany closed her eyes tight and huddled in the corner of the cage, unable to do anything but brace for impact.

Chapter Four

Bethany awoke with a violent intake of air, as if she had been holding her breath. Chances were high that she had. It took her a second to realize that she was no longer in the cage and she was no longer about to be crushed by a giant wave. She took another deep breath and immediately regretted it as she caught the first whiff of dog breath.

"Gross," Bethany said, as she turned to find herself face-to-face with Rufus. He began wagging his tail as he whined and then let out a small burp.

That got Bethany moving. She was out of the bed in one swift roll and slide. Thankfully, the burp wasn't a harbinger of more vomit. Rufus was standing now, still wagging his tail. It was exponentially more energy than Bethany could muster at the moment.

Rufus hopped off the bed and pranced out of Bethany's bedroom door, turning back to see if she was following. Bethany looked at the clock. It was 6 AM. She was typically an early riser, but she felt exhausted at the moment. Sleeping in a bit was appealing, but, then again, that dream had been terrifying. Regardless of her feelings, she had to care for a doggie.

It's just a couple of days, Bethany thought, trying to convince herself it wouldn't be so bad. She followed Rufus down the hallway.

The kitchen opened into a fenced-in backyard. The day was already lightening up, but Bethany still turned on the outside light. She let Rufus out while she brewed coffee. He pooped right away, and she grudgingly put on her shoes to go out and bag it up and place it in the outside trash bin.

"Good boy," Bethany said as she patted his head. "Do you want some breakfast?"

Apparently, Rufus wasn't quite ready to come inside to eat. A squirrel attempted to cross the yard while Rufus wasn't looking, but his eye caught the movement and he was off, running the squirrel up a large oak tree in the back of the yard, barking and wagging playfully.

Bethany left him to it. He'd come to the door when he was ready, and chasing squirrels might help deplete his energy. She had things to do. She grabbed a cup of coffee, taking a couple of sips while watching him from the outside doorway.

What a life a doggie has, she thought. So simple. Most days it seemed like she sorted through each moment like an eternity.

The backyard had a nice wooden, four-foot-tall privacy fence. Rufus should be fine. He was still occupied with the squirrel. She decided to have breakfast and check out what Jenna had sent her before going into surgery.

Bethany felt a bit ragged from the dream, but decently rested now that she was up and moving around. She had had strange dreams when she was younger, especially when she was learning her gift, but it had been a long time since she had something that felt so real.

Bethany took her coffee, her one vice, and some toast and sat at the kitchen table with her tablet. She opened up a browser and searched for "what does tsunami in a dream mean?"

Her eyes widened at the repeated references to major life transitions, fear of the unknown, strong emotional conflicts, big changes.

She wasn't sure how much credibility she gave to dream interpretation, but it also was somewhat inline with what happened at the grocery store. Meeting her future husband was a big deal. Losing access to her safe room was an even bigger deal.

She thought about the other parts of her dream. They were all trips down memory lane, but she didn't like what they showed her about herself. She was a coward with Lana. She manipulated

Jenna into doing work she didn't want to do. And she held herself back from opportunities that might have connected her to other creative people.

What's done is done, she thought. *I can't undo it.*

However, she didn't feel good about it. That could be an emotional conflict. Bethany felt like she might be heading down a rabbit hole, trying to piece together some meaning from the dream. She didn't need a dream to tell her she had a fear of the unknown. As for as the dream went, she wasn't sure there was more for her to know.

The next thought was of Dream Guy and how she had let him get away. She still needed to figure out why seeing him had interfered with her gift. She wondered if he had a gift, too, and maybe they short-circuited each other. That thought amused her. She drifted back into the feelings of the safe room vision and how wonderful it felt. That was better than the disturbing nature of her dream.

Rufus barked, and that brought her back to reality. She needed to focus for a little while. There was actual work that needed to be done for the day. She could always daydream later.

Bethany went through her personal reminder list, checking off things she had no intention of doing, but didn't want to see on her list all day. They were all really great things to do, things the books she read recommended, and she was sure they would even help if she did them. Her failsafe was that she had created her reminder list to keep them popping up each day. One day she would check off them all.

At least there was nothing major to deal with. After breakfast, she would start her routine bookkeeping work and then shift into whatever Jenna had sent her before she went into surgery.

She opened up her shared work calendar with Jenna to see what was on the agenda later, but glanced out the window just before looking at it. She was just in time to see Rufus scaling the back of the fence and disappearing over the side.

"Oh, crap!" Bethany shrieked as she dropped her phone and bolted outside. "RUFUS!" She ran to the side gate and dashed out and around the house towards the street. She caught sight of him crossing over the asphalt and cheerfully running down the sidewalk towards the cul-de-sac at the end of the road and the trailhead that led into the county park.

Cursing under her breath, she ran after him, still in her pajamas. At least she still had her shoes on. She called out as she ran to catch up with him. He turned to see her and then ran faster, as if this was some sort of game. Any hope of catching him before getting to the path disappeared.

"CRAP!" Bethany cried as she entered the path and ran to keep Rufus in her sight.

"Rufus, come back!" she whispered-yelled, realizing she might disturb the neighbors that were probably still sleeping.

As she bounded down the path, she was grateful that it was early, as she didn't see anyone else on the trail. It wasn't her ideal way to start the day running through the woods in her thin pajama-pants and a T-shirt. Up ahead, she could see where the path opened into the main part of the park. Dogs were not supposed to be off leash. And she realized she didn't even have a leash with her.

Too late to worry about that, she thought. *I can't lose Rufus.*

The county park was small, with a paved trail that went around a medium-sized lake. It's where Bethany usually got a run or jog in. In the afternoon, it was typically full of people getting in some light exercise.

Bethany was perhaps thirty feet from the opening when she smashed through a large spider web stretched across the path. She had a moment to see the silhouette of its spindly body as she caught the web right across her face. She yelped as she halted long enough to pull at the web and attempted to brush off any possibility of the spider being on her.

Bethany felt something on her arm and saw it crawling along her forearm.

"Get it off!" she shrieked, then realized no one was around and she was going to have to remove it. She blew on it a couple times and it hunkered down on her arm and held on more tightly.

"Oh, my God!" she said through clenched teeth. She looked around for something to work with and picked up a stick. She held it close to the spider and forced it to climb on it so she could put it down and get back after Rufus.

"Why-why-why?" Bethany asked to herself as she began running along the trail again.

As she exited the wooded path from her neighborhood, she could see the parking lot. A half dozen or so cars were already there. The sun was mostly up now, and she could see people out on the trail.

Two ladies were power walking up ahead. Bethany scanned the area for Rufus. To her dismay, she spotted him coming out of the pond. He usually hated water, but she saw he had had enough time to terrorize some ducks that were making a quick swim away. He gave a triumphant bark when he saw her. Bethany walked over as quickly as she could, worried that if she ran, it would make him run again and draw more attention to the situation than she would like.

"What I am going to do with you?" Bethany said as she knelt down in front of Rufus. He shook off the excess water on his fur, and Bethany had no time to avoid getting pelted with mud and pond water. Rufus barked cheerfully again and jumped on Bethany to play. However, it threw off her balance and her feet slipped out from under her and she landed roughly on her rump in the muddy patch she had been standing on at the water's edge. To make matters worse, Rufus bolted off again.

"WHHHHHHYYYYYY!" Bethany threw her arms up in supplication to the Universe.

"This your dog?"

"At the moment, he's a pain in my -" Bethany stopped. Something about the voice was familiar. She turned to see a man wearing a weight-vest squatting and giving Rufus cuddles. She recognized him immediately as Dream Guy. "Uh…"

Bethany jerked herself to attention. This was not how she envisioned seeing him again. Had she even envisioned it? That jostled her enough to try to tap into her gift. Still out of commission.

"Organic food girl," he said as she turned to him.

So he had a name for her, too?

"Is this getting close to nature part of your lifestyle?" he said. It sounded playful and not snarky. Strangely, it helped ground Bethany a bit—as did actually being on the ground.

"Is that how you burn off all that junk food?" Bethany said, almost without thinking, pointing at his weight vest. He smiled.

"I suppose. I'm Marcus, by the way," he said.

"I'm Bethany," Bethany responded automatically. She had a name now. She wondered if there was a subtle way to get his last name, too. At least then she would have a better lead. She attempted her safe room once more, and it was still a no-go. She would have to find out as much as she could without it.

"I've seen you twice in two days. Did you just move here?

Goddess Game

"No," Marcus said, giving Rufus some cuddles. Rufus pawed at him to continue when he stopped. "Just visiting."

Marcus glanced around the park. Bethany wondered if he was bored with her already and she tried to think of something to say. Several people were walking by and staring at her. She could also see more people pulling into the parking lot.

Before she could think of anything else to ask, Marcus gave her and Rufus an assessing look. "Do you need help?"

The reality of the situation sank back in. Bethany could feel the coldness of the mud on her buttcheeks through her thin pajama pants. She could only imagine what she looked like with water and mud splatters from Rufus.

Bethany felt herself tense up at the prospect of that kind of attention. She suddenly couldn't think about Marcus or the dream life or making a stronger connection with him. Bethany could feel more and more eyes on the three of them, like laser beams. She hadn't been prepared for that.

"I've got to get out of here," Bethany said. She stood, feeling the back of her pajama bottoms drooping heavily with wet dirt. The elastic waist was doing its job for the time being.

"Hey, do you have a leash for your dog?" a voice asked.

Bethany realized she had to get moving. She looked at Marcus, wishing she could think of anything else to say. She had to get Rufus out of the park, though. Bethany could feel eyes on her from every direction now that she and Rufus had been called out even further.

"Thanks for holding him," Bethany said. "I've got to get him home before we cause more of a stir."

"You have to have your dog on a leash in the park," a voice said, getting closer.

Bethany looked over to see a man stomping his way over to them.

"Sorry, I've got him," Bethany yelled. In one swoop, she bent down, wrapped her arms around Rufus's legs, and lifted all forty-five pounds of him off the ground, and bolted towards the path back to her house.

She didn't hear anything else from the voice and was glad of it. Rufus took it all in stride. Bethany was just about to the trailhead back to her neighborhood when she saw one of her neighbors, Anna, from two houses down, coming out with her baby in a stroller. Bethany nodded to her in acknowledgement as she approached to go around.

"Are you okay, Bethany?" Anna asked. She looked somewhat bewildered at the sight of Bethany and Rufus.

"Wonderful," Bethany said through gritted teeth.

As Anna rolled passed Bethany, the stroller wheel caught the edge of the bottom of Bethany's drooping pajamas and Bethany nearly fell forward with Rufus. She managed to hang onto him, but her waistband did not hold on to her waist. Bethany heard

Anna gasp.

This is not happening, Bethany tried to tell herself.

But it was.

Bethany put Rufus down as stoically as she could manage, holding onto his collar lightly as she yanked her pants up. She didn't dare look behind her. She hoped no one was watching, especially Marcus, but who wouldn't be watching the woman with muddy pajama pants carrying a dog out of the park? That's when she also considered what all the mud on her backside must look like right now.

"I-I'm sorry," Anna was saying. "Take this," she unclipped a strap from one of her bags on the stroller. "It looks like you need a leash."

Bethany took the strap. She felt like she was in a state of shock. She wasn't sure she had the energy to pick Rufus up again. Bethany suddenly wanted to take a long nap and not wake up for ten years or however long it would take everyone to forget this had happened. Maybe 100 years.

"Thank you," Bethany said. "I'll get it back to you."

"Whenever," Anna said. "We've all had days like that."

Bethany didn't think that was possible, but she nodded and turned towards home.

"Come on, Rufus."

Rufus walked back to the house as energetically as he had left it. Bethany, on the other hand, was reliving every agonizing moment of the last few minutes over and over. They arrived at the gate to the backyard. As Bethany closed it behind her, she bit her fist, trying to hold back the agonizing scream that wanted to escape.

Chapter Five

Bethany cleaned up Rufus and got him inside, taking extra care to towel off his muddy paws before letting him loose. He still left moist footprints on the kitchen floor, but at least they weren't fringed with dirt.

"I'm going to need you to up your good boy game," she said to Rufus. "I'm not impressed. Though you did cause me to run into Marcus again," she said. "Marcus," she said it slowly, considering it. "Good name," she said. "I wonder what Marcus is up to right now." She gave Rufus a few cuddles. "He could still be at the park." Bethany frowned. "Or he might be leaving the area. He said he was visiting. I wonder if he meant the area or maybe … he's visiting someone?"

Rufus rolled over, offering up his belly for a rub. Bethany gave him a couple of quick rubs.

"I should be mad at you," Bethany said. "I'm not sure we made a good second impression."

Rufus twisted his body back to a laying position and looked at her with his head cocked to the side.

"I've got to stop talking to a dog and actually make this day normal again," Bethany said. She looked down at her mud-splotched clothes. She could feel that the mud across her bottom was drying and flaking onto the floor. "I'm still a mess."

First things, first. She needed a shower.

She left Rufus in the kitchen and made her way through the house toward her bedroom. This house truly felt like a sanctuary. She often thought of it as her safe room in the real world.

The walls held echoes of her childhood—patches of slightly different colored paint where she had drawn on the walls, her height on each birthday notched on the outer trim of her bedroom's doorframe.

Inside her room, she paused in front of a family photo framed on a shelf. It showed her parents sitting on the front porch, their faces bright with laughter as a young Bethany hugged them from behind, one arm around each parent, pulling their faces close to hers on either side. She'd been maybe seven or eight. Her father had passed just a few months after that photo was taken. The memory sent a familiar ache through her chest.

Bethany thought about what her dream had shown her. What

Goddess Game

would her parents think of what she had done with her life? With her gift? She smiled longingly at the image of the three of them smiling. Life was so much simpler before her gift showed up.

Bethany grabbed a quick change of clothes and went into the bathroom and saw herself in a mirror for the first time since coming in. She was disheveled, but it wasn't as bad as she imagined. She let the muddy clothes drop in a pile on the floor, turned the shower on hot and hopped in to rinse away as much of the embarrassment of the morning as possible.

As she relaxed under the steamy spray of water, her mind ran through everything that had happened. She was really kicking herself for not making more of her second opportunity to talk to Marcus. It was almost as if both situations where she encountered him were engineered to make it hard on her.

"Aargh!" Bethany lightly pounded the shower wall with her fist, then turned off the water. Whether or not she was ready for it, life went on. She dressed and checked in on Rufus. He was still lying on his dog bed by the window in the sun, snoozing as if nothing unordinary had occurred.

If only it were so easy. It was time to get the day back on track. A typical day in the life of Bethany Hart went a little something like this:

1. Wake up. Some light stretching. Coffee. Breakfast.
2. Clear bookkeeping tasks (this usually took up 3-4 hours of the day).

3. Lunch. Maybe some exercise before eating.
4. Shift into illustrating, working until 4-5 PM.
5. Dinner. Maybe some exercise before eating.
6. Reading or streaming shows.

Predicable. Safe. There were no random dog chases or angry ladies on motorized carts, and, sadly, there were no dream guys.

Bethany shook her head side to side to stop any further detours of the mind. She couldn't think of anything she could do about the situation at the moment, and if she began going down that rabbit hole again, nothing would get done.

Instead, Bethany jumped into her daily bookkeeping work. It was something she started doing in college to earn extra money, and it had turned into a steady job. She could work from home online and earn enough to pay the bills. She would have loved to illustrate full time, but sometimes it took Jenna a while to find her work and she wouldn't even know where to begin to find work on her own.

It worked out pretty well. At first, Bethany felt like the bookkeeping kept her mind sharp, but it became routine. She went through the motions of keeping everything up to date. It seemed like work anyone could do.

Illustrating still made her smile even though it wasn't steady work. She'd had some repeat work from publishers, but more often the work was coming from people that were self-publishing. The main issue with that was that most authors just wanted to pay up front and not have to deal with royalties. That made the project more costly and many would just go find a cheap illustrator online.

That's the way of the world, though. The work that went into being able to stand out and get attention was daunting. Doing what you loved and hoping to find people that liked it was a slow game, if even possible. It seemed intimidating and impractical. At least Bethany got to work on illustrating projects occasionally.

Bethany was always a little sad when one project ended and she was waiting for Jenna to do her magic and make another appear. She wasn't sure how Jenna did it. Jenna seemed to know everyone and to be a part of everything.

Jenna lived with Bethany, but more often than not she was out and about meeting with people, going to conferences, and whatever else helped get her on the pulse of various creative jobs. Bethany wasn't her only client—just the one she was closest to.

Bethany sat at her computer and pulled up her schedule of bookkeeping tasks for the day. She grabbed her phone to put it on vibrate while she worked and noticed that she had several missed calls from the same unknown number, one within the last two minutes. She never heard it ring because she had her phone silenced for non-contact calls. The person hadn't left a voicemail.

Bethany was about to delete the calls and block the number when she felt compelled to open the work items that Jenna had sent her. It seemed like ages ago when she first tried to open it just before Rufus made his escape.

She opened up the shared calendar, and she saw that the missed calls matched the client contact Jenna had listed for Bethany to call. Something about the name was familiar, but Bethany was too shocked to focus on that. Her eyes widened in alarm. Why would Jenna ask her to call a client?

The whole client-contact piece was Jenna's side of the partnership. Bethany hadn't considered that Jenna would expect her to do that. She thought that maybe the list would be something like pulling together a portfolio of a certain style of drawings or some quick sketches. Surely actually talking to a client could wait until Jenna was available. Bethany felt her inner whiny kid throwing a tantrum.

I don't want to! It cried, accentuating the point with a couple of foot stomps and folded arms.

"WHHHHHYYYYY?" Bethany cried out to the Universe once again. No response. She was starting to think the Universe was ghosting her.

Bethany growled to herself. Rufus, already snoozing on his dog bed in the kitchen, opened his eyes, gave Bethany an annoyed look, then closed his eyes and began snoring softly after a few moments.

"That's right, ignore me, Rufus," Bethany said. "I'm just mad because NOTHING is going my way."

Goddess Game

Bethany glared at her phone, but was also torn because she had told Jenna she would step up. Whether she liked it or not, this was where Jenna needed her to step up. She opened the contact, and, after a few moments of hesitation, saved it. She really didn't want to, though.

Bethany opened up her text messages. She wondered if Jenna would be awake. Maybe she would be feeling better than she thought. Bethany began rationalizing a solution. Truthfully, without her gift operating, it wasn't the best idea for Bethany to engage in a conversation that could end up with her losing a job for them. Surely Jenna wouldn't want that.

As Bethany began tapping out a message, the doorbell rang.

Rufus sat up as if he hadn't been actively snoring moments before and ran towards the door, barking.

Bethany followed cautiously and looked out a nearby window. Maybe Marcus had been so smitten by her that he followed her home? Perhaps he liked dirty girls…

Shut up, overactive (and weird) brain, Bethany thought as she peeked out around the blinds and curtain. Bethany was relieved to see Jenna's mom. She opened the door.

"Ms. Finch, hi," Bethany said and gestured for her to come in. "How's Jen?"

"Could you put the dog away somewhere?" Ms. Finch asked, looking around Bethany at Rufus wagging his tail in delight at a new person to give him cuddles. His optimism was admirable, but in this case, not rewarded.

"Of course," Bethany said. She led Rufus to the nearest room, which was her office, and closed the door. Bethany returned, and Ms. Finch took a tentative step inside, pulling a mask up and over her mouth and nose. "So, Jen?"

"She's finally getting some much-needed rest," Ms. Finch said. "Still, she insisted I come over and get her laptop. Between you and me, she's not working today. She just had surgery. There is no reason she can't take at least a day or two to recover like a normal human being. Right?" she asked, her eyes narrowing at Bethany.

"Right," Bethany said in a small voice.

"You know, Bethany," Ms. Finch went on. "I've often felt that you take advantage of my Jenna. She does more for you than for anyone else."

"We help each other out," Bethany said defensively.

"Hmph," Ms. Finch grunted, looking around without stepping further into the house. "Where's her laptop?"

"Oh, yeah," Bethany said. "I'll go get it." She dashed over to the desk in the living room where Jenna often worked when she wasn't on the go and grabbed the laptop and cord, stuffed it in the bag hanging from the desk chair, then made her way back to Ms. Finch.

"Ah, thanks, I guess," Ms. Finch said. "You know, it really will do

Jenna good to have a change of environment. Maybe she'll see she has more potential than what she has here. I always thought her talents would go further in a bigger town or city."

Bethany was silent. With her gift was on the fritz, silence seemed better than saying anything that she was currently thinking to Ms. Finch.

"I'll text her later to check in," Bethany said and then clenched her mouth shut before anything else came out.

"If she doesn't respond, she's resting," Ms. Finch said as she walked to the door and out. "Bye, now."

"Goodbye," Bethany said with a forced smile as she closed the door and leaned against it with a sigh. "Today can't get any w-"

Bethany didn't dare finish. Saying it out loud was dangerous and could call forth more calamity. And she just remembered that she had put Rufus in her office and closed the door.

Bethany's mouth felt dry as she walked over to open the door and let Rufus out. Her mind was painting all sorts of images of destroyed furniture and equipment. Had it really been a good idea to close Rufus up in her sacred creative space? She held her breath as she pushed the door open.

Bethany was relieved to see everything seemed intact. Rufus sat in the middle of the floor, wagging his tail. The only thing out of place was her old black expandable portfolio bag. It looked like Rufus may have pulled it out from its resting area between her desk and work table.

"Were you thinking that would be some tasty fake leather, boy?" Bethany said as she walked over and patted Rufus on the head. At least he hadn't done anything more than pull it out. He got up and bounded out of the room.

The weight of what was happening in her life was almost too much to bear. Bethany felt even more helpless now. How could she text Jenna and prove Ms. Finch right?

She grabbed the portfolio bag and lifted it up on her desk. She hadn't used it in years as she had moved on to mostly create in a digital format, but it held a lot of memories. As she opened it, something tickled at her mind.

"I dreamed of you last night," she said, remembering the part of her dream where she had never submitted her drawings to her college publication. The portfolio was stuffed pretty tightly with paper drawings.

Bethany pulled out a stack of papers of various sizes and weights and textures. It had been fun to experiment with different mediums when she was younger. She smiled at some caricatures she had from college, similar to the one in the dream.

Bethany came across a couple of pages that had a storyboard for a children's story she had come up with after college. The story seemed a little lame, but the sketches were cute. A drawing of a fairy-godmother type character caught her eye. The mischievous side-eye and confident stance made her think of the woman in her dream, even though she hadn't seen what she looked like.

She did not want to think about the dream any further right now. She had things to deal with. Bethany pushed the drawings back into the portfolio and gently let it slip back into its familiar position by the desk, but she didn't push it all the way to the wall. Maybe she would take her time looking through it later.

She sat in her room and took it all in. Her desk and work table were on the right side of the room when you stepped inside. On the back wall was a double window that brightened the room up when she opened the blinds. On the other side of the room was a bookshelf with copies of books she had worked on, a nice, big rubber plant, and a cute little meditation nook that Bethany felt she should use more often.

Despite her best effort, now that her portfolio had triggered memories of the dream last night, her brain was conjuring up even more scenes in her life where she had used her gift to avoid conflict or use people to get what she wanted. It had essentially been her way of life since her teens.

She wished she could put these thoughts away in the same way she had put away the portfolio. They persisted, though. Now that she was remembering it all, she realized that there must be a connection between the dreams and her gift not working. Maybe she was being punished because she used it selfishly. Or maybe it was always going to stop at some point.

It also was peculiar that her gift would stop when she felt like it would make the biggest difference. If she was to trust her gift, and she did, she just encountered the man of her dreams (visions) twice and she had gotten no closer to making it a reality.

Bethany walked back towards the kitchen to get her phone. There was nothing she could do about her gift (or lack thereof), but it didn't mean she was going to waste the day.

She opened up the message she had begun to Jenna before her mom showed up and backed it all out. Rufus was back to snoozing already.

As Bethany contemplated her next move, her phone rang. She looked down, and it was the contact she had just added. Bethany dropped the phone on the table like it was a viper about to strike.

Chapter Six

Bethany stared at her phone ringing and vibrating on the table. She eyed it like a haunted artifact in a horror movie. You don't touch something like that. Curiosity leads to danger. You don't open yourself to the possibility of bad things happening, right?

She desperately wanted to let it go to voicemail, but was conflicted by her desire to be a good friend to Jenna. She was also worried that if she didn't answer it, they would both lose work. And, for Bethany, the work Jenna brought in was the type of work that fed her spirit and made the more boring aspects of her life bearable.

Bethany reached for the phone and hesitated. She didn't know what this person wanted or if she could even help. Jenna had indicated nothing about the call other than it was scheduled for today.

As her finger hovered over the green "Accept", Ms. Finch's accusations about Bethany using Jenna echoed in her mind. Memories of the dream had singled out how Bethany had manipulated Jenna to do the things that she didn't want to do. It was slightly possible she owed it to Jenna to take a little weight off her shoulders.

Bethany took a deep breath, accepted the call, and put the phone to her ear.

"This is Bethany."

"Is that how you answer the phone? This is a business number, isn't it?" The voice on the other end was sharp and authoritative.

"I...." The no-nonsense tone of the caller took Bethany by surprise. She thought identifying herself was an appropriate way to answer a call. "I guess it's both."

"You guess? Well, that's professional," an annoyed and disappointed sigh. "Well, be glad you answered, because this was going to be my last attempt to reach you. I thought I would be talking to Jenna. Why did she give me your number at the last minute?"

"I'm sorry. Jenna had a medical emergency," Bethany said. She put the phone on speaker and placed it on the table so she could fully wring the nervousness out of her hands. It didn't help. "What can I help you with, Ms....?" Bethany struggled to remember the name she had just saved on her phone.

"Didn't you know I was calling? This is Meredith. Meredith Stoker." Silence for a few moments. "What's that echo sound? Am I on speaker?"

Bethany quickly took her off speaker and held the phone up to her ear again. She felt like a kid again. A kid on a winning streak of not getting anything right.

"I'm sorry," Bethany began and was interrupted.

"It's probably for the best. I'm not a fan of going through gatekeepers, though it makes me wonder why people think they need to be kept."

Bethany didn't know what to say to that.

"Look, you have me on the phone for a limited time." Ms. Stoker sounded more impatient now than at the beginning. "Is there something you want to tell me?"

As Bethany took a deep breath to regain some composure, the name finally clicked in her mind. For the first time since the call began, she had enough presence of mind to try to enter her safe room. She was still denied. She almost burst into tears.

This wasn't just any client. This was THE client that Jenna had been talking about for months. She had mentioned Ms. Stoker on several occasions. Bethany had half-listened, knowing that Jenna would handle any progress she made. The potential to land Ms. Stoker as a client was a big deal. She was prolific in creating well-received children's stories and she had made a name for herself by bringing on little known illustrators for each new story and giving them an opportunity that usually led to more illustrating work for them.

Jenna had even tried to show Bethany articles and blogs about Ms. Stoker in various children's book venues. Bethany gulped. There was much more at stake than she had realized when she accepted the call.

"Ms. Stoker, yes," Bethany's voice squeaked. She cleared her throat and fumbled her way forward. "I admire your efforts to highlight new illustrators with your stories." That sounded good. She could make words. She tried a few more. "Were you considering using me to illustrate your next book?"

"Me consider you?" Meredith laughed for several seconds. Bethany frowned. "Jenna reached out to me. Said I should have a look at your work. I did. I admit your drawings are nice. I want to know about *you*."

"Me?" Bethany made another effort to go into her safe room. It still wasn't working, but it had been worth a shot. This didn't feel like it was going well—except for the fact that Meredith liked her work.

"Yes. I want to know who you are as a person. If my chat with Jenna had gone well, we would have been talking, anyway. It will help me decide."

Bethany's brain was spinning. What had Jenna gotten her into? This woman didn't need to know her for Bethany to illustrate her books. Ms. Stoker was coming across as really pushy and

Bethany didn't like that.

"Decide?" Bethany asked, trying to stall as she attempted to think of a way to extricate herself without causing problems for Jenna.

"Do you think you're the only illustrator I'm looking into?" Meredith asked. "I want to know why I should choose you."

"So I am being considered?" Bethany said without thinking. She cringed when silence followed.

"Perhaps," Ms. Stoker said. Bethany thought she sounded amused. "Again, I'd like you to tell me why I should consider you."

Bethany was back to square one and beginning to get miffed that she was having to navigate this without her gift. As a last attempt to get through the conversation in a positive way, she tried to think through times when her gift was available. There had to be a pattern to the paths that led her where she wanted to go. She didn't know Meredith or enough about her to know what she would value.

"Well?" Meredith said into Bethany's contemplative silence. "Are you still there?"

"Yes, I am," Bethany said. She was getting more and more irritated at Meredith's abrasive personality. She wanted more illustrating work, but maybe this wasn't a good fit. Bethany decided to stop trying so hard and just let things fall out how they would.

"To be honest, Jenna didn't have a chance to fully update me on your project, so I apologize for not being more prepared. As for me as a person and as an illustrator. There's nothing more I love in the world than drawing pictures that make other people smile."

For a second time, Meredith didn't have a quick response.

"Very well," she eventually said.

"Very well?"

"Let's meet," Meredith said. "The next stage is an in-person meeting. It's hard to hide who you are when you have to look someone in the face."

"Um…," Bethany wasn't sure what to say. The last thing she wanted to do was meet this woman. The only reason she hadn't blurted an immediate "no" was because she really did want another illustrating job. She also considered that Jenna would probably need more income to help offset the cost of what her health insurance did not cover for the surgery.

"There's no 'um' about it," Meredith said. "I have five other calls to make, and I've wasted a lot of time trying to reach you. Why aren't you asking me for meet-times already? Don't you recognize what this opportunity could mean?"

The conversation was going too fast for Bethany to keep up. She was back to being terrified about making a misstep. She switched Meredith to speaker again and pulled up her calendar.

"When is a good time for you?" Bethany asked in a small voice.

"Better," Meredith replied. "Actually, it looks like the only time I can fit you in is tomorrow afternoon. I must make a decision by the end of the week so I can stay on schedule. Do you like coffee? Let's meet for coffee."

"By the end of the week?" Bethany repeated.

"Yes," Meredith said. "Time's a wasting. Are we meeting or not?"

"Great," Bethany said, trying to sound enthusiastic and failing. She wasn't expecting it to be so soon. She hoped it could be next week when Jenna would be healed enough to go.

Without her gift, this woman would eat Bethany alive. She at least needed a safe place to meet. And an opportunity to assert some control.

"Would you be okay meeting at the coffee shop in the new bookstore, Bookmarked? It's in the Plaza with the Village Pantry."

"Hmm…," Meredith considered it. "I have been wanting to check that place out. And I love supporting local. Let's do it. Two o'clock. Tomorrow. Don't be late."

And with that, she hung up.

"Guess we're meeting at two tomorrow, then," Bethany said to her phone. She added a reminder to her calendar and tossed her phone back on the table.

"Don't you dare ring again," she said to it and then jumped when it buzzed. Thankfully, it was just a reminder to do laundry.

Bethany paced in front of the kitchen table a few times, reviewing the conversation and seeing if there was any way out of the meeting. How big of a deal was this Meredith Stoker?

Bethany grabbed her phone and sat at the table. She performed a search on Meredith and all the articles and blogs and mentions that she remembered Jenna talking about came up. She really was a big deal. All illustrators she worked with went on to get more work because of the connection to her stories.

That would be great for her and Jenna. And, after she got started on the project, she shouldn't have to be in contact with Meredith. She would have Jenna to be the go between.

Still, she wasn't sure what to expect from the meeting and how she should prepare. Forgetting about letting Jenna rest, Bethany texted Jenna and asked if she was up for a call. Soon the phone was ringing.

A groggy Jenna answered.

"You've got about ten to fifteen minutes before the pain meds kick in and I'm asleep."

"I'm sorry, Jen," Bethany said. Maybe she did take too much advantage of her friend. Here she was, calling to complain to her while she was trying to recover. "Are you in a lot of pain?"

"It's mostly sore," Jenna said. "I don't think I'll need the pain meds after today. Rufus doing okay?"

"Ah, yeah, Rufus is fine," Bethany said. She didn't want to go into the whole morning fiasco.

"And Meredith? Did you call her?"

"She actually called me," Bethany said. Her mouth went dry just remembering it.

"Oh," Jenna was quiet. "You okay? I wasn't expecting her to do that. I just gave her your number so she would recognize it when you called her." Jenna yawned. She really sounded like she would fall asleep at any moment.

Bethany wanted to ask why she thought that was a good idea, but it didn't seem to be the time to go down that path.

"We're meeting tomorrow," Bethany said with a sigh. "I'm sorry to bother you while you're healing. But what do I need to do?"

"What did she say?" Jenna asked. Her voice was alert as if the news had cleared the medicative mind-fog a little.

"She wants to get a feel for me?"

"Then, just be yourself," Jenna said, sounding relieved. "You can talk to people."

"I thought we wanted this job," Bethany laughed weakly.

"You can do this," Jenna said. "I've been meaning to push you towards being more involved. Now that we're older, it makes me nervous that you depend on me to be your liaison with the outside world." She yawned.

"Really?" Bethany said. She wondered if the pain medicine was causing Jenna to be more honest than she might be otherwise.

"You can do this," Jenna said again. "Or I can meet with her next week," she sighed. "Whatever."

"Tomorrow is the only time. She's making a decision by the end of the week."

"Hmmm…." It sounded like Jenna was drifting off.

"Okay," Bethany said, almost more to herself than the half-asleep Jenna. "You keep healing. I've got this."

"Yep, bye," Jenna said with another long yawn, and then the call ended.

"Why?" Bethany put her head down on the table.

She didn't even have the frustration to yell it out to the Universe as she had earlier.

Chapter Seven

For the next hour, Bethany paced the kitchen while thinking about the meeting with Meredith. Even though she usually thought of her house as her sanctuary, it was beginning to feel like the walls were boxing her in. Her heart was pounding like she had just finished a run. Her body, accustomed to exercise and responding to the nervous energy, wanted to move.

She glanced over at Rufus. He watched her anxiously from his dog bed.

"Want to go for a walk?" she asked.

Rufus's ears perked up.

"Let's go."

Bethany walked to the front door. Jenna had all over Rufus's gear ready to go. She took his harness down and he took his position at the door, waiting patiently as she slid it over his head and snapped it together around his torso. She clipped the leash around her waist and attached it to the harness, then checked to make sure the little zippered wristlet on the leash had a few poop bags in it. These tiny actions to prepare for going out gave her mind something different to focus on for a few moments.

She stood with Rufus at the door, wondering what her plan was. Where would they walk? Rufus looked up at her expectantly.

"You're right," she said, and Rufus wagged his tail. "Let's just get out of here and see how it goes."

Bethany opened the door and stepped outside into a beautiful, sunny afternoon. She looked down the road to the trailhead to the park.

"Not going that direction," she said to Rufus and began walking in the opposite way, where they would head down the roadside on sidewalks. She wasn't sure how far she wanted to walk, but moving in any direction already felt better than being inside the house.

Bethany and Rufus walked down sidewalks through several nearby neighborhoods, only slowed by Rufus's curious sniffs. Bethany still had energy to burn, so they continued their stroll and eventually came to the shopping center with the Village Pantry and Bookmarked. She let Rufus lead her along the walkway in front of the bookstore.

"Rufus!" Caleb burst out of the door with open arms, and Rufus jumped up for cuddles. Caleb looked at Bethany, his expression friendly but carrying a hint of concern. "I saw you two coming off the sidewalk. How's Jenna?"

Other than the concern, Bethany noticed he looked relaxed and confident. She had the feeling of seeing him for the first time in a long time.

"Uh, the surgery went well," Bethany said when she realized she hadn't answered. "She's healing now. She's been discharged and is staying at her mom's house for a couple of days."

Bethany rolled her eyes at the mention of Ms. Finch.

Caleb nodded. He was eyeing her in a peculiar way. Bethany wondered if she had something on her face.

"I'm glad it went well," he said. "How are you?"

"Me?" Bethany forced a laugh. "I'm great. Why would I be otherwise?" She managed a smile. It felt more like a scowl.

"Yeah, well, that wasn't remotely convincing," Caleb said. His tone was gentle, but direct.

"What do you mean?" Bethany asked dumbly.

"You seem a little distracted and nervous," Caleb said. "You're usually more unreadable. But, if you must know, your neighbor Anna stopped by."

"What?!" Bethany exclaimed. The events of the morning came

flooding back. She wasn't prepared to relive that embarrassment so soon. "Did she really?"

"Yeah." Caleb nodded. "She did. I don't know if I should laugh or commiserate. Which one are we doing?"

"Why would she come to you?" Bethany asked, throwing her hands up. So much for a walk making her feel better. The thought of her neighbor blabbing to her ex-husband escalated the whole matter to another level. Who else had she told?

Caleb shrugged.

"You're not always approachable, Beth," he said. "And she knows we were... that we are good friends."

Bethany nodded and looked down, noticing a piece of gum smashed flat on the concrete. It had the dark marks of footprints on it. She felt a little like that at the moment, like life was walking all over her and she was getting squished and hardened by all the pounding. The gum was holding up pretty well, though it was marred a bit. She wasn't sure she felt the same about herself.

"I know," Bethany said when finally she looked up. Caleb was watching her closely. She scrunched her face as the fullness of her embarrassment hit her once more. It seemed like a lot had happened since the morning of Rufus shenanigans. If there was any positive takeaway from the day, it was that as problem after problem showed up, the ones she couldn't do anything about seemed like less a big deal.

"I guess if that is the worst that comes of it, I'll be doing okay," Bethany said with a sigh. She realized she had bigger, looming problems to worry about. "What a crazy day."

Caleb tried to keep his face straight, but then he burst out laughing. It was contagious, and after a surprised moment, Bethany laughed, too.

"It's not funny," she said, though she continued to laugh. "I was mortified."

"Were you really wearing star-bangled underwear?" Caleb snorted.

Bethany felt her face go red. That detail was very specific. Caleb laughed harder. The sound reverberated off the store windows. When the laughter had run its course, he invited her to come inside.

Bethany held up the leash.

"Thanks, but preoccupied."

She was also considering if she should move away and change her name.

"Rufus can come in, too. I'm the boss, remember?" Caleb smiled. His concern was clear and genuine. Bethany felt her defenses crumbling.

"It feels like you're being a little bossy." Bethany elbowed him playfully as she led Rufus inside. She was desperate to talk to someone and with Jenna medicated and everything else going on, Caleb was the next best option. He had always been good at helping her sort through her thoughts, even if he didn't know about her gift.

The bookstore's interior welcomed them with its familiar fragrant blend of paper, coffee, and wood polish - scents that made Bethany feel at home. A few customers browsed the shelves, their movements creating a peaceful rustling in the background.

"Aunt Beth!"

Startled, Bethany turned to see a familiar, but much-changed, face. Her eyes widened when she recognized who it was.

"Katelynn?"

Katelynn waved excitedly from behind the counter. The last time Bethany had seen her, she had been only twelve - all gangly limbs and braces. Now she was practically grown, the awkward preteen transformed into a poised young woman. The sight made Bethany's heart twist with all the time that had passed, all the family moments she'd missed.

"Why are you looking so grown up?" Bethany asked, walking over to give her a hug. The gesture felt natural, even though technically their relationship had ended with the divorce. "How is school? Are you close to graduation already?"

"Yep," Katelynn said with a grin that reminded Bethany so much of her younger self. "I've been learning to draw better. I'd love to have you look at my work sometime."

"Sure," Bethany said. "That sounds awesome." It felt nice to still feel accepted as almost family. The bonds formed over years of holidays, birthdays, and ordinary moments hadn't been wiped out of existence with the signing of papers. "We'll get something worked out. I know where to find you now."

"Yay!" Katelynn's enthusiasm was infectious.

"Wow. They really grow up fast," Bethany said to Caleb.

"I know," he responded with a heavy sigh. He turned to Katelynn. "You've got things for a minute?"

"Sure," Katelynn said. There were only a few people in the coffee shop and a couple in the bookstore browsing. Another person was manning the coffee shop. Bethany thought she saw Katelynn give a conspiratorial wink to Caleb, but he just shook his head slightly.

"All right. Let's go somewhere we can talk," Caleb led Bethany and Rufus through a door at the back of the store that opened into his office and a storage area beyond.

The office space was both familiar and new to Bethany - she'd helped set it up when the store first opened, but now it had developed its own lived-in character. Caleb had placed a desk to one side, while a comfortable seating area with a couple of plush chairs occupied another corner.

He'd even created a small kitchenette-type area with a sink, microwave, and small fridge, as well as a table and chairs for breaks. The storage area beyond was in a state of chaos, with opened boxes and cardboard everywhere.

"Ignore the mess," Caleb said, gesturing at the storage room. "We're switching up some displays and putting out new books this evening."

Rufus settled at Bethany's feet as they both sat down at the small table.

"You really made this happen." Bethany looked around in admiration. In all the years she'd known him, she wouldn't have guessed he would choose this direction for his life.

"Yeah," Caleb said with a note of pride. "You want something to drink?" He reached over and opened the fridge and grabbed a bottled water for himself and offered Bethany one. She waved it away.

"No, thanks," she said. She enjoyed the comfortable silence between them as Caleb opened his water and took a sip. "This is nicer than our first apartment."

Caleb smiled, nodding.

"Doesn't take much to hit that mark," he said. "If we had stayed there longer than we did, we would have probably gotten divorced sooner."

They both laughed, but Bethany's laughter felt forced. The fact that they might have gotten divorced sooner hit a little too close to home for her. Caleb did not know how much she had manipulated outcomes with her gift throughout their marriage.

"True," she said. The rest, as always, was left unsaid.

Caleb closed his water bottle and leaned forward on the table. It wobbled slightly.

"So?" he prompted.

"So," Bethany repeated, then shrugged. She felt a certain degree of comfort with Caleb that she wasn't sure she deserved. "I'm just realizing that I don't know how to do this."

"What? Talk about what's going on with you?"

"Maybe," she said, reaching down to pat Rufus, grateful for an excuse to break eye contact. "I don't feel … composed."

"Ah, yes, the Bethany Hart composure," Caleb said.

"What does that mean?" The question came out sharper than she intended.

"I think you're right," Caleb said. "You do normally seem composed on a regular basis. I've actually wondered how you do it. It's like you dance through life with everything falling into place."

"Hmph," Bethany grunted. She'd never considered how it looked to other people. Had he noticed this pattern during their marriage? She had spent so much time in her safe room during those years, using her gift to smooth every interaction. Some memories from that time were a blur of careful manipulations and avoided confrontations.

"I think this is the first time I've seen you out of sorts," Caleb said. "And that whole park display this morning is not typical Bethany Hart territory."

"I know," Bethany groaned. "Everything feels wonky and out of control today. I don't understand it."

"Have you considered the wonky stuff is just growing pains?" Caleb asked, gently.

"I'm closer to menopause than puberty, Caleb," Bethany said dryly.

"I don't mean physical growing pains," he chuckled. "Sometimes life can feel a little unwieldy when you're learning to manage more. I definitely feel that way on a day-to-day basis right now. But I love it because I get to become better at what I want to do."

"So this is how the normies live?" Bethany murmured to herself.

"What?"

"Just kidding," Bethany said. "I guess I thought I had my life managed nicely."

"What's different? Or is anything different?"

Bethany didn't answer right away. She wasn't going to tell him about Marcus or her gift. He might think she was going crazy.

"I don't know," she finally said, looking down at the tabletop and scratching at what turned out to be an imperfection in the printed top. "I suppose I'm not as happy with my life as I thought. I'm not sure what to do about it."

She could feel Caleb looking at her. Their shared history suddenly felt like it was filling the room with unanswered questions. Terrified at what might follow the silence, Bethany reached out for her gift like someone falling from the top of a building and only able to grasp air.

Bethany casually wiped a tear from the corner of her left eye, hoping that Caleb hadn't noticed. He was watching her so closely. It was up to her to break the silence first.

"I'm too young to be having a mid-life crisis, right?" she asked, adding a halfway convincing laugh at the end. She grew more serious when he didn't laugh. His expression was concerned. "I'm sorry. I don't really mean to sound melodramatic. I -," she began, trying to boil it all down. "I'm scared," she finally blurted, surprising herself.

"I know how that can feel," Caleb said. "Do you want to talk about it?"

She did, and she didn't.

"It's okay if you don't," Caleb said after an extended silence. "But whenever you are, I'm here for it."

"Thanks," Bethany replied softly, then remembered about her meeting tomorrow. "There is one thing that is freaking me out that I'm not sure what to do about."

"What is it? Maybe we can brainstorm solutions?"

"If only there was a solution that didn't involve me," Bethany said.

"Well...?" Caleb leaned in. "Can't help if I don't know what we're up against."

"Argh," Bethany grumbled. "I have a meeting with Meredith Stoker tomorrow."

"Meredith Stoker? That's awesome," Caleb said. "Isn't it?" he added when Bethany didn't seem to agree.

"We're going to be here tomorrow at 2." Bethany put her head in her hands on the table.

"Here? At the bookstore?" Caleb was trying not to sound eager and failing.

"The coffee shop," Bethany said as she lifted her head and dropped her hands. "And this is serious! You know I don't do this in-person meeting stuff. She's not a nice person. She's super pushy and Jenna won't be there. I feel like I'm going to lose my mind." Bethany put her head back in her hands again.

"Okay," Caleb said. "I think I understand." He pointed at her as he spoke. "You are doing something that you're not used to doing and your brain is making you think it will be a disaster. Close?"

Bethany frowned, but nodded yes.

"We all go through that," Caleb said. "Haven't you done something before that you thought would be scary and it turned out okay? You probably even learned something from it?"

Bethany didn't respond at first, but remembered when she started kindergarten and she didn't know anyone. That was before her gift and she went into it like all the other kids. Looking back at it, they were all figuring out how to go through the day and learn stuff. And she enjoyed school.

"I suppose," Bethany said.

"It sounds like you're on the hook for this no matter what," Caleb said. "Maybe you can prepare yourself, so you go in feeling a little more confident."

"How am I going to do that?" Bethany said.

"Well, what are you afraid might happen?" Caleb offered. "Anything in particular?"

"I don't know," Bethany said. "It's possible I have a panic attack or pass out or some other unforeseeable catastrophe."

"Or, you just have coffee and answer a few questions?"

"I don't know," Bethany said. She could see Caleb was right, but she was still nervous.

"How about this?" Caleb went on. "I'll keep an eye out and if anything looks like it's getting out of control, I swoop in and cause a distraction?"

"Hmmm...," Bethany eyed Caleb. "How would you do that without making it awkward?"

"Are you kidding? It's Meredith Stoker and I have a bookstore. There are tons of things I could come up and say to her to take the heat off you."

"Interesting," Bethany said. "That actually does make me feel a little better. I like having a plan." She smiled at Caleb. "Thank you."

"Since we're stretching comfort zones, let's take it further. I started a game group a few months ago. We meet at my house on Fridays to play cards or board games. We have enough people to split up and do different things. I think you would like the people there and I would love for you to come. It's a standing offer. No pressure. We start at 7 PM."

Before she could respond, the office door opened and Katelynn walked in. Rufus came to attention.

"I need your help out here," Katelynn said to Caleb. "Sorry..."

"No worries," Bethany said as she stood. Rufus followed suit. "Thanks for the chat. Guess I'll see you tomorrow..."

"You two still look good together," Bethany heard Katelynn said as she walked away. "I was hoping I'd walk on you smooching."

Bethany got out of the store before she heard anything else.

Chapter Eight

Algebra II class. Freshman year. Bethany was dreaming again.

She felt more aware in this dream, as if she now knew what to expect. This was her first memory of connecting with her gift. She had been daydreaming while the teacher was breaking down a long problem on the board. She was disturbed out of her reverie when the teacher, Ms. Dewitt, hit a snag and asked the class if anyone could see where she had gotten off track. A few students went up, trying to figure it out.

And that's when Bethany saw where Ms. Dewitt had made a mistake. She had brought down one of the numbers with the wrong sign and that had messed things up. Bethany became nervous as she considered raising her hand. Several of the other smarter kids in class hadn't seen it. They were so competitive. Would they be mad if she pointed it out? At the same time, she saw the answer, they didn't, and why wouldn't she help the teacher?

Time slowed, and she found herself in the safe room for the first time. She didn't call it that when it first happened, obviously. She thought maybe she was daydreaming again, but it seemed more real. The white wall in front of her showed the video clips that she was now familiar with, but it caught her off guard the first time. After a few moments, she realized that she could stop and start them with her mind.

She let several of the videos play out and she realized she didn't like any of the attention she would get from raising her hand and giving the answer in front of the class. Bethany sort of intuitively knew that she was seeing possibilities. She finally saw one that she was okay with. She focused in on that one.

Once she had made the selection, young Bethany found herself back in class as if no time had passed. After the bell rang with no solution to the problem, Bethany hung back as the other students left the classroom. She then walked up to Ms. Dewitt and pointed out the error. Ms. Dewitt slapped her forehead in exasperation.

"Ugh. I can't believe I did that," she said. "And then I couldn't see it. Nobody else did." She looked at Bethany. "Why didn't you share it with the class?"

Bethany shrugged.

"I just wanted you to know, so you'd know," she said with a

shrug, and walked towards the classroom exit. The door slammed shut.

Bethany turned, surprised. This part had never happened. Ms. Dewitt's demeanor had changed. She stood a little taller, seemed more matter-of-fact.

"You're not getting away that easily," Ms. Dewitt said.

Bethany looked back at the closed door and then around the classroom. The only other door was in the back, and that led into Ms. Dewitt's office. The classroom had windows, but they were those unusual ones that opened at a slant. Bethany wasn't sure where she would go if she wanted to escape.

Right now she was just in an empty classroom with her old teacher, or some dream-person who looked like her teacher. It wasn't exactly scary, but strange and disconcerting.

"This is what I just don't get," Ms. Dewitt said, *walking over and sitting down at her desk. Bethany looked over at the closed door, wondering if she should see if she could open it. No one else was in the classroom but Ms. Dewitt and Bethany, and Bethany was a little curious about what was happening.* "Some extra-dimensional power leaked through to your little third dimensional life," Ms. Dewitt went on, "and you decide to hide instead of using it to accelerate your growth."

"What?"

"Look, I know being born human gets your perceptions all muddled. It's not easy for sure. But why are you calling out to me and still not doing anything to help yourself?" Ms. Dewitt said.

"What are you talking about?" Bethany asked. This dream had the feel of the safe room—like it was really happening, but not in the physical world. "Who are you?"

"Don't you recognize your math teacher?" Ms. Dewitt said with a mischievous grin. "You were once good at solving problems."

"You're not Ms. Dewitt," Bethany said. "What's going on?"

"Oh, my, you found me out," Ms. Dewitt said with mock surprise. She stood up, her body glowing with a whitish light as she transformed from a squat, stoutish 50-something woman to a tall, beautiful statuesque goddess with long, dark hair. Her skin continued to glow, changing to a bronze color as a sleek, white dress appeared. The glow faded to a normal skin tone, but she still emanated a light all around the outside of her body.

"Who ... are you?" Bethany asked, a little taken aback by the power of this person's presence. "This is a dream, right?"

The woman placed the palms of her hands together like praying and looked down, as if trying to decide where to start.

"What is a dream?" the woman asked, head still bowed. "An opening? A place of learning? A homecoming? Surely, it's a mystery?"

When she looked up, Bethany felt the full force of her gaze. It was like a jolt of energy passing through her and beyond. Bethany felt her body vibrating and buzzing. It was startling and *weird, but it also felt ... right... and safe.*

"Who are you?" Bethany asked again when she was able.

"I won't be able to fully answer that," the woman said. "I may not answer a lot that you would ask. Just know that I am your greatest ally. For now and always."

Bethany couldn't take her eyes off the woman. Something about her seemed so familiar. She couldn't place what it was. She still wasn't sure why, but she felt a trust that made little sense under the current circumstances. It was as if she trusted this woman as she would trust herself. Bethany then remembered something her mom had said—that she would always be with her to guide her.

"Mom?" Bethany asked.

The woman smiled, but shook her head side to side in the negative.

"No," she said. "Unless you consider we are all one." She held Bethany with another long gaze before speaking again. "I know your mind is struggling with this experience. Call me Fiona."

"Fiona," Bethany repeated. Bethany's mind was having a hard time grasping what was happening. She was having a light and fuzzy, dreamy feeling. Which made sense because she was dreaming.

Bethany was clear that she wasn't awake. This was a dream. This was her dream. Maybe Fiona was some access to her subconscious, some avatar for her higher self. She held onto that thought as she determined how to best make use of this situation. Perhaps she would have access to some answers.

"Why is my gift not working when I need it most?"

Fiona chuckled.

"That's all you," she said, taking a step towards Bethany. She pointed to a nearby student desk. "Have a seat."

Bethany found herself sitting in the middle desk at the front of the classroom.

Fiona began walking slowly back and forth across the front of the classroom, watching Bethany. As she passed Bethany, Bethany could feel the same warm, fuzzy feeling of safety and power flowing over her as if from Fiona's gaze.

"Let's work this out, shall we?" Fiona began. She continued to walk and watch Bethany as she spoke. She pointed to the dry erase board and a stick figure with 'Bethany' written over it appeared. "Here you are." Fiona looked back at Bethany. "What's the next piece in this equation?"

Marcus flashed through her mind. Bethany looked down at the desktop. Someone had drawn a screaming lady in the upper right corner. It seemed appropriate. She knew what Fiona was getting at, but she didn't want to play along.

"The sooner you participate, the sooner we can move on. You can't keep anything from me, Bethany," Fiona said.

"Okay," Bethany sighed. "I met this guy and my gift went on the fritz and showed me that we would be married. But everything has been crazy since then and I don't even know his last name or where to find him."

Fiona nodded. She pointed to the board. Another stick figure with 'Marcus' written over it appeared to the right of the Bethany-stick figure. A plus sign appeared between them.

"Did you like what you saw in that vision with him? Do you want that life?" Fiona raised an eyebrow.

"If I can't hide anything from you, then you should already know."

Fiona chuckled again and pointed to the board. An equal sign appeared next to the Marcus stick-figure and on the other side of the equation was the Bethany and Marcus stick figures sitting in a tree, kissing.

"Very funny," Bethany said. "Look, I don't know why this is happening, but I don't see how this is helping."

"I suppose this equation isn't really complete," Fiona said. "I left out one variable."

She flicked her finger at the board again. To the left of the Bethany figure was a swirl that looked like a clip art, one-color galaxy-swirl. The Bethany figure and the galactic swirl were next to each other as if being multiplied.

"Guess that changes the outcome, huh?" Fiona shrugged.

On the other side of the equation, Marcus and Bethany were no longer in the tree. The Bethany figure was standing alone, surrounded by stick figure cats.

"I'm more of a dog-person," Bethany muttered.

"Do you understand what is going on here?" Fiona asked, ignoring Bethany's comment.

"Is that swirly thing supposed to be my gift?"

Fiona nodded yes.

"So, if it is a part of the equation, it messes up my chances of having a life with Marcus?"

Fiona shrugged.

"I don't know. I'm just creating visuals for you. Is this what you think the problem is?"

"Well, it was my gift that showed me that life, so that conclusion doesn't make a lot of sense."

"But there is a connection?" Fiona asked with an innocent smile.

Bethany looked at the equation. Something didn't feel right about i, but she couldn't see it. Her gift was a part of her. Should it be separated out like that? Wouldn't it be on both sides of the equation?

Just as she thought it, the swirl appeared on the other side of the equation with Bethany, balancing it out. Marcus and Bethany appeared in the tree again.

"Ha!" she said.

"Oooh, you've sorted out something," Fiona clapped. "But…." The word lingered.

"But?"

"Doesn't seem like you're balanced at the moment, does it?"

"My gift isn't working." Bethany looked down at the desk again, thinking through what had happened already in the dream. She looked up at Fiona. "Did you say I called you?"

"That's right," Fiona said. "Think of me as your guardian angel if that helps. And, so you know, this conversation is more real than you know. Dream or no dream."

"Guardian angels help people, right?" Bethany asked. "Are you going to help me with this? Why isn't my gift working?"

Fiona looked at Bethany for a long time.

"You cheated," Fiona said. It was a statement of fact, no judgement in the words. Bethany was about to argue when Fiona elaborated, "And by that, I mean that you cheated yourself."

"How did I do that?"

"Your gift," Fiona said. "There are consequences to you using it the way you have."

"What other way was there to use it? It helped me have a better life," Bethany said.

"You think you have a better life?" Fiona asked.

Bethany was about to respond in the affirmative, but she thought about how angry she was at having to repress her real feelings all the time. She also thought about the life she had envisioned with Marcus. It was leagues better than her current life, which wasn't terrible, but also not the best.

"That's right," Fiona said. "Your avoidance of messy situations also meant that you didn't learn what you needed to learn to do what you came to do."

"And what was that?" Bethany leaned forward in the desk, gripping the front edges.

Fiona laughed.

"I won't help you with that," Fiona said. "You have to figure some things out on your own."

"If you really want to help me, I would love to get my life sorted out again. If my gift was working..."

"That's the whole point of it not working," Fiona said.

"Why? So I can have a mental breakdown?" Bethany leaned back in the desk and slumped down.

"I know it may seem confusing," Fiona said. "The good news is that you have inadvertently created life habits that have helped you stave off some karma you would have accumulated otherwise. It could be so much worse."

"Worse?" Bethany frowned. "You say I cheated. What was I supposed to use my gift to do?"

"Your gift," Fiona smiled. "You are barely scratching the surface of what is possible. But to answer you honestly, you could have chosen the paths that would help you learn your lessons faster. You could have leaned into your discomfort. Even if you didn't choose a path, you could have learned from the unwanted consequences in the others you saw just by feeling what they were like," Fiona said.

"You could have helped others on their journey if they were open to it. You chose a different way." Fiona shrugged. "If you are not where you want to be in life, it is on you to change it." Fiona leaned in. "Because if you don't, that brief vision you saw with Marcus will never happen. You are not ready for it and won't be able to make it happen. It will be thwarted no matter what you do."

Bethany noted how Fiona seemed amused by her frustrations and wondered aloud, "By you?"

Fiona sighed.

"By you," she said, pointing at Bethany for emphasis. "Again, you're in control of your own life."

"Was that you in my last dream? Someone took the key to the cage. It was you, wasn't it? You took the key and said something about your move. Is this some sort of game?"

"Life is a game, Bethany," Fiona said. "Do you even know how to *play it?"*

That stopped Bethany for a moment.

"You better figure it out fast," Fiona said. "The clock is ticking. In a couple of days, it will be decided by default."

"What's that supposed to mean?"

"This particular opportunity will disappear by the end of the week if you don't make some changes."

"And why is that? Am I going to die?"

Fiona smirked.

"Wait. Am I?" Bethany's eyes widened as she bolted upright in the desk.

"No," Fiona said. "But third dimensional existence is a funny thing. You all are bouncing and bumping against each other. You've made contact with this person and a potential life path that you are interested in, but his bounce is taking him away ... unless you somehow do something to intercept it or draw him back in. If he leaves before you make a connection, he may choose another path. He has that choice for his own life. You don't get to decide for someone else. If you miss him now, your next shot will be in the next life. If you don't mind waiting..."

"I don't even know how to find him," Bethany said sullenly. The comment about not deciding for someone else felt like a jab to the gut.

"There is more operating here than your physical existence," Fiona said. "Surely you realize that by now."

"Can you tell me where he is? What should I do?"

"Do you have better questions?" Fiona asked, stone-faced.

Bethany felt like she was flailing at figuring this out. What would be a better question? After several moments, she made another attempt.

"How do I get the life I envisioned?" she asked.

"More of what you just did to start," Fiona said. Bethany frowned. "Be present. Assess and respond. Don't you know you are capable?"

"I just wanted a quiet life," Bethany whispered.

"But you really don't," Fiona replied. "I know that. You know that. You've seen the life that you want. Was that vision you had worth some uncomfortable effort?"

Bethany considered it. It was worth that.

"What do I need to do?"

"Don't you know yet?" Fiona said. "Isn't your life showing you?"

"My life is showing me that I'm not fit to operate without my gift." Bethany mumbled.

Fiona stared at Bethany for several long moments.

"What?" Bethany asked. Fiona's scrutiny was intense.

"What, indeed," Fiona said. "I think you just need a few nudges in the right direction."

"I don't like the sound of that."

"Yeah, you probably won't like it," Fiona said. She began walking away. The classroom changed into a forest with a cave opening into what looked like space, with stars shimmering in vast darkness.

"Where are you going?" Bethany asked. She tried to get up from the desk and found she couldn't move.

"My turn, again," Fiona said, without turning around.

Bethany was about to respond when the dream shifted and she found herself back in the cage, hanging over the cliff. She actually screamed as she turned and saw the giant wave coming. NOT AGAIN!

This is a dream, Bethany thought. I can control this. She squeezed her eyes shut, imagining the wave disappearing. She opened one eye, then the other. To her surprise, the wave was gone. She laughed in relief.

"Maybe I've got this," she said to herself.

She looked at the cage and grinned. She walked over and opened the door and after a few awkward attempts not to fall, she closed her eyes and levitated up and over to safety on top of the cliff.

Outside of the cage and without the stress of the wave coming, Bethany realized that the view was breathtaking. Since she was still dreaming, she considered what else she might want to do while she was in control.

As she imagined possibilities, she turned to see the wave was back and not only back, but moving faster and already almost upon her. She saw something moving along the water's surface—giant sharks gnashing their teeth. She barely had time to brace herself before the wave crashed down on her with full force.

Chapter Nine

Bethany awoke with such a violent start that she fell out of the bed, landing face first on the floor. Luckily she had a rug that took some of the edge off the hardness. Not much, though.

She pushed herself up and looked at the clock.

"Geez," she said as she forced herself to stand. "Fiona is kind of a bitch."

Now, I believe my dreams are real. Sheesh, thought Bethany. But she also didn't discard the idea. Too much strangeness was happening lately.

Rufus walked in to see what all the commotion was. His nails clicked against the hardwood floor as he approached, head tilted in curiosity.

"You again," Bethany said with a sigh. The early morning light cast long shadows across the room, making everything feel slightly surreal after her intense dreams. "Guess you want to go potty and have some breakfast?"

Rufus barked and wagged his tail, and began walking towards the kitchen, looking back to make sure Bethany was following. His enthusiasm for the simple routines of life was almost enviable. She walked outside to watch him, not wanting a repeat of the day before. The morning air was crisp, carrying the scent of someone's fresh-cut grass from down the street.

He went potty and, thankfully, came back into the house for breakfast. Bethany gave him his grub and made her own breakfast before thinking about the day. The main thing on her calendar was Meredith, and she didn't know how she was going to prepare for that. Luckily, she had Caleb in her corner when everything went down.

To delay thinking about it, she grabbed her phone and opened a browser to search for "lucid dream with a person I don't know talking to me." It was a wordy search term and she was sure she'd have to try a couple of different variations, but several intriguing interpretations showed up.

One reflected a thought she remembered having in the dream. It suggested that her subconscious was trying to communicate something, some hidden aspect of herself that might need more investigation.

"Fiona, Fiona," Bethany mused aloud while absently stirring her coffee. The spoon clinked against the ceramic mug in a steady rhythm. "Are you some part of me?"

She read a bit further about self-reflection and yada-yada-yada.

This wasn't getting her work done. To clear her mind and her to-do list, Bethany got herself ready and jumped into her bookkeeping tasks for the morning. It was soothing to do something that either required little thought or, if anything was off, resolving the issues was a very specific troubleshooting process. Anything more complicated could be escalated to the accountant or business owner.

She was so laser-focused on her work that she got through all of it before lunchtime. Thankfully, she was paid by project and not by the hour.

Afraid to eat anything too heavy before meeting Meredith at 2 PM, she made a protein shake and paired it with some pretzels. The shake was a pale green from the spinach she'd added. Thankfully, she had added enough fruit and maple syrup to counteract any bitterness.

At this point she was playing a waiting game and if she didn't find something to do with the time, she was going to go bonkers making up terrible things that could happen.

Her phone buzzed with a text from Jenna: "Good luck with Meredith! You've got this!"

Bethany smiled weakly at the encouragement. She wished she shared Jenna's confidence. As the minutes ticked by, her anxiety grew. She paced the kitchen, rehearsing potential conversations in her head. If only she had the certainty of her gift back.

She drove her cute, little green Kia Soul instead of biking or walking. No need to add sweatiness from physical exertion into the already volatile mix of things.

The drive to the coffee shop felt both too long and too short. Bethany parked and checked her reflection in the rearview mirror, tucking a stray strand of hair behind her ear. She took several deep breaths, trying to center herself.

You can do this, she told herself. *Just be professional. No weird episodes today.*

The coffee shop was busy with the afternoon crowd. The buzz of conversation and the hiss of the espresso machine filled the air. Bethany ordered a coffee, hands only slightly shaking as she paid, and found two comfy chairs at a table that weren't being used. She had brought in her tablet, so she sat down and began sketching to avoid talking with anyone.

"I don't want to do it," a voice said, probably a young male.

Bethany realized it was coming from the person sitting at the table behind her. She tried not to listen, but she couldn't help it. It sounded like her own internal conversation.

"Why did you change your mind?" another voice asked, another male, but older. "I thought it was a big deal for you."

"Why do I have to have reason?" the first voice said. "Can't I just say no and not have to think about it anymore?"

"I guess," the other person said. "You can do whatever you want. I suppose the better questions I can ask are: What do you want? And what are you willing to do to have it? If you're committed to what you're doing, you need to at least evaluate things based on whether it will get you closer to what you want or not. And it's fine if you don't want to do one particular thing. But you are going to have to take actions to get what you want."

"I know," the first voice said. He sounded tired.

Bethany didn't hear the rest as two ladies sat down on the other side and began chatting as they knitted. Bethany decided to mind her own busy and focus on what she was drawing—a kid-version of herself going to school on the first day.

"Are you Bethany?"

Bethany looked up, startled to see an older woman. She recognized the face from the articles she had read up on. Meredith was early as well. She wore a crisp navy blazer and carried herself with unmistakable authority.

"Yes," Bethany said, her voice higher-pitched than normal.

"I thought I recognized you from your online picture."

Meredith sat down as Bethany stood to greet her and shake her hand. She sat back down, a little embarrassed. The chair made an awkward squeak.

"It's, uh, nice to meet you," Bethany said. "Thank you for

meeting me here."

"It's really a cute little bookstore and the coffee shop seems nice," Meredith said. She looked down at Bethany's coffee mug. "I see you've ordered. Mine should be on the way."

Meredith fixed her with a stern gaze. Why did everything feel like school lately? Bethany almost raised her hand before speaking.

"Should we wait for your coffee?" Bethany asked. It seemed like a dumb thing to say, but it got the words flowing again.

Meredith waved her hand dismissively.

"I'll get it when I get it. Let's talk about you." Meredith leaned forward on the table and narrowed her eyes. "How did you get into illustrating?"

At least that was a simple question, though Bethany did try to tap into her gift. As she was coming to expect now, it was still not working.

"I have always enjoyed drawing, especially silly and fun stuff." Bethany said. She looked around to find Caleb. She needed to make sure he knew she was already under siege. "It was easy to translate that into illustrations for children's books."

"Hmmm...," Meredith leaned forward. "Do you have children?"

"No," Bethany said.

Meredith tapped her fingers on the table and leaned back.

Bethany finally located Caleb, but he wasn't looking her direction and she had no good way to get his attention.

"Hmph. Tell me about your business arrangement with Jenna," Meredith said. "Will I have to access to you or will I have to go through her for everything?"

"Uh…," Bethany wasn't sure how to answer to ensure this would go smoother. She remembered Meredith had mentioned not liking gatekeepers, but she should have some say in it as well. Bethany didn't want to be at anyone's beck and call. She tried her gift again, knowing it still wouldn't help. She decided to just answer as honestly as possible. "Jenna typically manages all contact. I can be open to some contact, but prefer it to be email or using some other cloud service."

"I prefer meetings like this at specific parts of the process. That's why I always choose a local person or someone within the state. Are you willing to do that?"

Bethany felt like the answer should be yes to get the job, but she didn't really want to say yes. She tried her gift again, straining her eyes to try to shift inward. She needed this conversation to go in the best way. And if her vision said she had to say yes, well … she would do her best to find one that worked out without that outcome.

"Are you okay?"

Bethany realized she was actually scrunching her eyes as she tried to trigger her gift. As she forced herself to relax again, she felt her gaze slip into her safe room for a moment, but instead of seeing this situation play out, she found herself in the middle of an extremely intimate moment with Marcus—all bare skin, rhythmic movement, and heavy breathing. What was worse than being distracted by the images playing out in her mind was that her body responded as if she were experiencing it all in real time. Bethany panicked.

As much as she had wanted to get into her safe room the past two days, she shifted out of it as quickly as she could. However, the physical reaction was already happening. She couldn't stop an orgasm that was growing more and more until it began its crescendo throughout her body.

The intensity caught her completely off guard. The pleasure rolled through her in waves, making her grip the arms of her chair. The chair squeaked again. At least she hoped it was the chair and not her!

"Oh, my God!" the orgasm continued. Bethany melted into her seat, unable to control the sensations rippling through her body even with the realization that she was in a public place and this should not be happening. The busy coffee shop suddenly felt too warm, too crowded.

She closed her eyes, trying to stop it and at the same time not wanting to stop it. The sounds of the coffee shop - the whir of the grinder, the clink of cups, the murmur of conversation - seemed to fade away, replaced by the rush of blood throughout her body.

Bethany felt arms around her, and she opened her eyes to see Caleb. He was carrying her off to the safety of his office. The movement only intensified the sensations. He placed her in one of the plush chairs. The fabric was cool against her flushed skin.

"Are you okay? I thought you were joking about having to be rescued," he said.

"Oh, my GOD!" Bethany said breathlessly. "I'm okay. It's just…" she felt another orgasm coming on. Her toes curled inside her shoes.

"Bethany, I recognize your O-face," Caleb said. "What is going on?"

Bethany allowed herself to experience the full orgasm this time. The pleasure was overwhelming, making her arch slightly off the chair. Thankfully, the feeling began to subside and fade away as it was replaced by the reality of what had just happened. She became acutely aware of every sensation - her sweaty palms, the lingering scent of coffee that had followed them from the shop, the distant sound of customers browsing the bookstore.

Her breath came in short gasps as she tried to compose herself. The embarrassment began creeping in, making her cheeks burn even hotter than they already were. Here she was, having just experienced the most intense pleasure of her life, on her ex-husband's office chair, in the middle of what was supposed to be a professional meeting.

"Is Meredith still out there?" Bethany finally asked, still a little breathless. She couldn't bear the thought of facing the woman after what had just happened. "Can you tell her I'm not well?"

"Are you not well?" Caleb said. "You seemed to be doing pretty well there." His attempt at humor only made her blush more.

"I'm sorry," Bethany said. "I can't explain what just happened, but I also can't go back out there. In fact, I will leave by your back door if that is okay." She started to sit up, then thought better of it, waiting for her legs to feel less shaky.

Caleb eyed her for a moment, his expression a mix of concern and amusement.

"I'll go talk to her."

Bethany sat in the office, the fullness of what had happened hitting her like the wave in her dream. This was even worse than the park fiasco. At least then she'd only lost her pants - this time she'd lost all dignity. The quiet of the office felt oppressive as she waited, every tick of the wall clock marking another second of her mortification.

Caleb came back, closing the door softly behind him. He had brought her tablet and put it on the table.

"I told her you'd be in touch but that you weren't able to finish the meeting."

"How did she take it?" Bethany asked in a small voice.

"I didn't give any other option," Caleb said. "She left." He shrugged.

Bethany put her face in her hands. So much for that job! Her fingers were trembling slightly against her heated cheeks.

"Did what I think just happened, happen?"

"Oh, my god…." Bethany said. This time, it was an exclamation of pure embarrassment. "How many people saw that?"

"A handful. I explained to everyone that you were okay. That no medical attention was needed. Is medical attention needed?" He raised an eyebrow.

"No!" Bethany said. "I think maybe a new identity is needed."

"These last two days have been more eventful for you than I have ever seen. Are you making up for lost time?"

"Can I please go back to a quiet life?" Even as she said it, she knew she still wanted the life with Marcus and wouldn't go back to how she was living before.

"If a little embarrassment is the worst that happens to you, you'll be okay. I know it may seem like a big deal to you, but most of those people will forget about this in the next few days. Most of them don't know what happened. They just saw you being carried off with a big, goofy grin on your face."

"I did not." Bethany threw the small pillow from the chair at Caleb.

"You definitely did," Caleb said. "I was a little envious."

"This is terrible," Bethany said. "I meant what I said about sneaking out. Can I hide out here a bit and leave out the back door?

"Of course," Caleb said. "Whatever you need."

Bethany managed a small smile. Despite everything, she felt grateful for his understanding and support. Even if she never showed her face in the coffee shop again, at least she still had people in her corner.

She lay back on the couch, staring at the ceiling as her breathing finally returned to normal. The incident had left her feeling drained but also strangely energized. Something was definitely happening with her gift, something beyond her control. The question was, what was she going to do about it?

Chapter Ten

Bethany waited around for another twenty minutes before sneaking out the back and heading home. She scurried across the parking lot with her head down and slipped into her car and got out as stealthily as she could manage. She wasn't sure she'd ever be able to look at the coffee shop the same way again.

When she opened the front door, she was surprised to see Jenna in the kitchen. She looked paler than usual and when she moved, Bethany could see she was being cautious. The appearance of Jenna had a dual effect of making Bethany feel relieved that she would have someone to talk to and also nervous about talking to her about what had just happened with Meredith Stoker.

"Jenna?"

"Bethany!" Jenna exclaimed. "How did things go with

Meredith?" Her voice was bright but strained.

"Why aren't you at your mom's house?"

"She was mothering me to death," Jenna said with a smile. "I'm still sore, but it isn't as bad as I thought it would be. If I put enough pillows on the couch, I think I can manage here just fine."

"That's good," Bethany said, watching as Jenna carefully navigated around the kitchen counter. "We'll just keep Rufus from jumping on you. Where is Rufus?"

"I let him out," Jenna said, pointing to the backyard.

Bethany quickly looked at the window to make sure he was still there. She could see him digging a hole a few feet from the fence, probably devising another escape route. All seemed well for the moment. She turned her attention back to Jenna.

"Is there anything I can help you with?"

Jenna side-eyed Bethany as she walked into the living room. Bethany followed close behind her with her arms out as if she could catch her friend if she somehow spontaneously fell in any direction.

"I'm okay," Jenna said, gently slapping away Bethany's arms, as she made her way over to the couch. "But I noticed you didn't answer about Meredith. You met with her, right?"

"I did," Bethany said, twisting her mouth up at the memory. "I did!" she said more forcefully when Jenna just stared at her.

"Well?" Jenna said. "I need to know how it went. Spill."

Bethany opened her mouth to speak, then shut it again. Then opened it. Where did she even begin?

"Was that job really that big of a deal?" Bethany finally asked. As tempted as she was, she didn't dare try to tap into her gift again. At this point, it was way too unpredictable. The memory of what had happened at the coffee shop made her cheeks flush.

Jenna narrowed her eyes at Bethany, her expression sharp and focused despite her physical discomfort.

"What exactly happened?"

"It—" Bethany began, but Jenna held up her hand.

"Let me sit down first," she said. She had already added pillows on one side of the couch and she slowly lowered herself down on the edge while holding the arm of the couch. She leaned back little by little onto the support of several stacked pillows behind her. "Now. Tell me everything."

"The meeting didn't last very long," Bethany said. She sat down on the edge of a nearby chair. "And I had to leave abruptly."

"You left in the middle of the meeting?" Jenna moved to sit up and then made a face as her midsection reminded her she was still recovering.

"Sort of. Technically, Caleb carried me off."

Jenna tilted her head as if trying to figure out a puzzle.

"How is Caleb involved?" she finally said.

"We were meeting at Bookmarked, over coffee," Bethany replied. The words were tumbling out now, and she hoped she could get through it without giving too much away.. "Meredith showed up early. Caleb was looking out for me to make sure I was doing okay and … next thing I knew, I was in his office."

"Are you saying you blacked out?" Jenna asked, her face scrunched up in confusion.

"I had some sort of … uh…collapse," Bethany said, studying the pattern on the throw pillow beside her to avoid meeting Jenna's eyes.

Jenna didn't say anything. She was staring at Bethany in stunned silence, her expression a mix of worry and confusion.

"So, are you okay?" Jenna asked with genuine concern.

"I'm fine," Bethany said. She looked away to avoid eye contact. "It was more embarrassing than anything."

"So, you didn't get to talk to her at all?"

"A little. She asked me about illustrating. She said if we worked together, she would probably want in-person meetings with me."

"Was that when the collapse happened?" Jenna asked jokingly. She shifted on the couch with a grimace, adjusting the pillows behind her as best she could without twisting too much. When Bethany didn't smile, she added, "Was it?"

"Yes," Bethany said in a small voice. "I'm sorry, Jenna. I really suck at the people-thing."

"You know, Bethany," Jenna began. She shifted on the couch again, causing another grimace. "It's weird when you say that because every time I've seen you interact with someone, you always seem to come out okay." She gave a small shrug. "That's why I wasn't worried about you meeting with Meredith. I've often wondered if you can you read minds or something."

Bethany felt her stomach drop. *Not exactly,* she thought. She never considered that Jenna had paid enough attention to notice that Bethany could get out of just about anything she didn't want. She needed to figure out how to do that with this conversation.

"Jenna, I'm really sorry I messed this up," Bethany said. "I'm not myself lately and everything seems to be happening all at once."

"You think you're the only one? Look at me." Jenna lifted her shirt and pointed at her sutures. "This feels like a nudge for me to take it easy."

"It doesn't look like you're taking it easy," Bethany frowned as Jenna moved more pillows around.

"I'm doing the best I can," Jenna said. "I'm used to going, going, going."

"You should take it easy, though," Bethany said, getting up and helping her friend adjust the pillows to her comfort. "You don't want to make it worse, do you?"

"Now you sound like my mom," Jenna said, rolling her eyes, but she smiled. She settled back on the pillows and sighed. "Thanks."

"No problem," Bethany said, moving back to her chair. "So, do you think I've ruined everything?"

Jenna mulled it over.

"Did you get any kind of vibe from Meredith at all? Did you have any feeling about how it went?"

Bethany gripped the arms of the chair tightly as the memories came back to taunt her.

"Not from Meredith."

"You're being a little weird, Bethany," Jenna said. "Did something happen that you're not telling me?"

"It's nothing," Bethany said. She didn't know how to explain what had happened without telling Jenna about her gift.

"I don't think it is," Jenna said. "I don't know how to say this without sounding weird myself, but I feel like this is the realest conversation we've had in years."

"Really?" Bethany said. She sat back in her chair, thinking about that. Jenna was her best friend, the person she was closest to, and she could tell that Bethany was holding back something.

Bethany mulled that over. That's not how she wanted their friendship to be. She wanted someone to talk to about everything that was happening to her. Jenna was the best candidate for that. Maybe they needed to have an even more genuine conversation. Maybe she should tell Jenna about her gift.

"Can I tell you something?"

"Oh course," Jenna said. She gestured to her throne of pillows. "You have a captive audience at the moment."

As Bethany deliberated on how to start, Jenna pointed to the door. Rufus was looking in on them.

"Could you let him in?"

"Oh, sure," Bethany said and opened the door. Rufus went right over to Jenna and jumped on the couch. Jenna had moved a pillow to act as a barrier. "Aren't you worried he'll jump on you and hurt you?"

"I suppose it's possible," Jenna said. She reached over the pillow and patted Rufus on the head as best she could. He turned and sat with his backside against the pillow. Jenna patted the pillow, too. "I trust him. And I create boundaries."

Bethany sat again and took a deep breath to clear her mind.

"What do you want to tell me?" Jenna asked.

Bethany considered how to begin in a way that would make sense. She thought over the years, trying to find an example to lead into the conversation. That made her think of her dream and that gave her a possible lead in.

"Do you remember when we were in high school and I had that idea about a story about a girl who could see various future outcomes? She could select the best one and live into that?"

"No," Jenna said. "But let's pretend I do. What about it?"

"It wasn't really a story idea," Bethany said slowly. She tried to gauge Jenna's reaction as she continued. "*I can actually do that.* I wanted to tell you then, but you didn't really believe me and I guess I have no way to prove it. After all these years together, though, you've seen and apparently felt the result of it. I come out okay in social situations because I can tap into some supernatural ability I have."

Jenna stared at Bethany. The silence stretched between them, broken only by Rufus beginning to snore.

"If it was anyone else, I'd think you were messing with me to see if you can get me to act crazy while I'm on pain medicine." Jenna glanced around. "I'd be looking for a phone recording this conversation."

"I don't make videos," Bethany said.

"I know," Jenna replied. She stared pointedly at Bethany. "And you don't lie or make up things to be funny."

Bethany looked down at her hands. She couldn't tell if this was going well or not.

"Also, I am not on pain medication today," Jenna went on. "I stopped to see how bad it would be. And it's not too bad." Jenna shifted slightly on the couch. "All that is to say that I am mostly clear-minded at the moment."

Bethany looked up at her friend.

"You believe me?"

"Let's just say I am open to hearing more," Jenna said.

Bethany nodded and moved to the edge of her seat.

"Okay. Like I said, I can see future outcomes. I go into my mind and sift through them until I find one that I want. Then I just have to select it, act it out, and things go the way I saw them."

"That sounds like imagination."

Bethany snorted.

"That's what you said when we were in high school, so I just dropped it. I've had a lot of years to experiment with it since then."

"Let's say I believe you," Jenna said. "Why didn't you try to tell me again later? Why wait until now?"

"I ... uh...," Bethany scrambled for a way to tell the truth that didn't sound as bad as the truth was. "It didn't seem important?"

"We're friends," Jenna said. "If this is true, we could have used it to bring in even more business. We-" Jenna stopped as Bethany pressed her lips together tightly. Jenna frowned as she realized what Bethany didn't want to say. "You didn't want to do that?"

"I mean," Bethany threw her hands up. "Weren't we busy enough?"

Jenna stared at Bethany, her expression unreadable.

"Okay," Jenna finally said. "Let me ask you this. How do you choose future you want to happen?"

Bethany hesitated. This is where things could get uncomfortable, but she had committed herself to having this conversation all the way out.

"I choose the one that works out in the best way for me," Bethany said quickly. "I'm not proud of that. It just…," Bethany wasn't sure what to say. "It just seemed like the best thing to do."

Jenna nodded and was silent for several moments before speaking again.

"If you really can see future outcomes and you choose the one that works out the best for you," Jenna said slowly, each word deliberate and careful, "Why aren't you doing it now?"

"I can't." Bethany threw up her hands again. "Something happened that same evening you had emergency surgery. Before you called me. My ability went a little haywire, and it has been out of control ever since. That's one of the reasons things didn't go well with Meredith. I was flying blind."

Jenna nodded again, as if she understood. This was going better than Bethany had hoped. Jenna spoke again.

"Do you know how many times I've wondered why I always end up doing exactly what you need, even when it's not what I originally planned?"

"What?"

"If I believe you," Jenna said, her voice growing harder. "Strangely, I actually think I might. It makes a lot of things make sense. Are you saying you've been manipulating the people around you all these years so you can do what you want to do?"

Bethany's eyes widened. She didn't want to answer, but the truth was already there, hanging out like her star-spangled underwear at the park.

"Well...," she began.

"And, more specifically, are you saying that you've been manipulating *me* all these years?"

"Jenna," Bethany moved over to the side of the couch.

"No," Jenna said, trying to push Bethany away, but her mobility was limited. "I want to know. I want you to say it."

"You're my best friend, Jenna," Bethany said, her voice cracking.

"Answer the question, Beth," Jenna said, her own voice tight.

Bethany tried to think of a way out of it, but couldn't. Finally, she answered.

"Yes," she said. "Though I feel like you've gotten something out of it, too," she added quickly, immediately regretting the defensive tone.

"Hmmm…." Jenna inched herself forward on the couch and leaned forward to slowly stand. Bethany got up to help her, but Jenna waved her away as if Bethany's touch was tainted with something unsavory. "Excuse me a moment." She walked over to the kitchen table, where she picked up her cell phone. After a couple of quick text exchanges that seemed to take an eternity, she turned to Bethany, who was terrified to say anything else, but finally managed to.

"Can we talk more about this?" Bethany said. "We're still friends, right?" The desperation in her voice was painful even to her own ears.

"So you say this ability of yours isn't working right now?"

"No," Bethany said.

"I guess if it was, we wouldn't be having this conversation. You'd still be using it on me." The bitterness in Jenna's voice was cutting.

"I don't use it on you…," Bethany started, but the lie died in her throat.

"We are supposed to be friends, Bethany," Jenna said, her voice rising. "You shouldn't manipulate your friends for your own gains. Do you have any idea how violated this makes me feel? How many of my choices weren't really mine?"

"Jenna, I…," Bethany didn't know what else to say. The truth had seemed like the right choice, but now she was watching her closest friendship falling apart before her very eyes.

"I texted Melody," Jenna said. "She's coming to get me and Rufus. I don't know if I can trust you," Jenna said. She shook her head in disbelief. "My mind is going over all the times you've gotten me to do what you didn't want to do. I even moved here and have been helping you with your bills."

"I thought that was a good deal for both of us," Bethany said, knowing how weak it sounded even as she said it.

"It might have been," Jenna said. "But you also knew I was thinking of moving. I could have had a completely different life right now. I won't know because I don't know where you might have nudged me to change my path." She wrapped her arms around herself, as if trying to hold it all together. "How many opportunities did I miss because you wanted me here, doing what was convenient for you?"

"I...," Bethany didn't know what to say.

"Don't bother," Jenna said. "Melody will be here soon."

Jenna didn't talk to Bethany while she waited for Melody. She went into her room and packed a light bag, her movements stiff with both physical and emotional pain. Melody came in later and carried it out for her, waving hello to Bethany, trying not to get involved in the dispute.

Bethany watched them leave, Rufus following and hopping in the car. The house felt empty. So did Bethany. The silence that settled over the house was deafening, filled with all the things she should have said, all the choices she should have let Jenna make for herself. For the first time, she truly understood the cost of her gift - not just to others, but to herself.

The door closed with a final-sounding click.

Chapter Eleven

Bethany awoke to a quiet house. No doggie nails clinking across the floor. Jenna wasn't just recovering at her mom's. She was gone. Bethany hadn't realized how much their presence made the house feel more like a home. She also realized that she was lying when she told herself that she was okay cutting herself off from people and being alone.

She stayed in bed a few minutes longer, thinking about how things got to this point. Should she have expected Jenna to get that angry? Bethany had selfishly expected Jenna to understand and be available for Bethany to vent.

I must be the worst person ever, Bethany said. *Jenna hates me. Caleb is the only person not mad and, if he knew what I did to him, he would probably hate me the most. Even my dreams have been kicking my butt for cheating at life.*

Goddess Game

That made Bethany try to remember what she had dreamed that night. She couldn't remember anything. Perhaps she had slept heavily, except she didn't feel rested at all. She felt like her life had been picked up and shaken violently, and she didn't know how to respond to that. Run away? Punch back?

Bethany slipped out of bed and went to the kitchen to start her morning coffee. The backyard was still dark, but starting to lighten. She wished she could take that as a metaphor for her life. A more accurate portrayal would be her life swirling down a drain and flowing out into whatever drains flowed out to. The ocean? The unknown? That seemed about right.

Even the kitchen felt desolate without Jenna's morning chatter or Rufus's eager face at the back door. It's not like Jenna and Rufus had never left the house or gone on trips. That had never felt like this. Like they might not come back.

Which was silly, right? Of course Jenna would be back—even just to get her stuff. That could be an opportunity to make amends.

The meeting with Meredith was probably beyond salvaging - who would want to work with someone who had to be carried off in a questionable state? Her illustration career might be over. Meredith would spread the word about her, and she wouldn't have Jenna to bring her work any more.

Bethany groaned. Life was hard when you couldn't easily choose the right path. It sucked not knowing how someone was going to react and not being able to find out what to do to avoid unpleasantries. And yet, she was seeing more and more clearly that even with how easy things had been using the gift, her life hadn't been satisfying.

Bethany realized that while she felt like she'd been wrung out emotionally, she also felt more calm, like surviving had taken some of the edge off the anger that had been building up inside her. She wasn't faking her way through everything. She was trying to be genuine. Well, maybe not trying, but that's what ended up happening.

With the list of odd things in her life stacking up, Bethany wasn't sure it could get any worse. Of course, that was a dangerous way to think. She had already lost her best friend, made her friendship with Caleb potentially awkward, ruined a business opportunity, and had no way of finding the person who had triggered it all—Marcus.

All this turmoil for a life she hadn't even known was possible until a couple days ago? Bethany sighed heavily, and then straightened up and banged her fist on the kitchen countertop.

Why was she beating herself up so much? She was doing the best she could under not-the-best circumstances. Bethany wondered if this was what most people felt like all the time. She had often admired the aloofness to criticism met by many others her age. Previously, she would have avoided any possibility of that at all costs.

She took a sip of coffee, her brain working furiously to sort everything out. Restless, she stood and wandered over to the door that opened into the garage. She wasn't sure why she felt

Goddess Game

inclined to glance out there, but her eyes were drawn to her bike. An idea began to form. She'd been passive for too long, letting her gift dictate her choices, waiting for life to happen to her. Maybe it was time to take action.

Setting down her coffee cup with newfound determination, Bethany got ready for the day. Instead of her usual work-from-home attire, she dressed for the mission at hand—a pair of bike shorts and a comfy T-shirt with a funny graphic of a killer whale eating other fish on it. It was quirky and fit her mood.

Back in the kitchen, she gathered some essentials into a small backpack - her tablet, a sketchbook, some energy bars, and a water bottle. She wasn't sure how long she'd be out, but she wanted to be prepared.

"Okay," she said to herself, checking her reflection one last time. "Time to make something happen. Time to find Marcus."

The morning air was crisp as Bethany wheeled her bike out of the garage. She had a loose plan - she'd start with the park where she'd last seen Marcus, then maybe circle through the nearby neighborhoods. He'd mentioned he was visiting someone in the area. Hopefully, he was still hanging around. She wasn't going to stumble onto him sitting around her house, so this was the next best option. She'd make herself available to be stumbled upon.

As she pedaled towards the trail to the park, Bethany felt a sense of freedom. This was the first time in years she'd done something without knowing the outcome. No safe room to guide her, no perfectly crafted script to follow. It was terrifying and exhilarating at the same time.

She hopped off the bike and walked it down the path to the park, then hopped on again and did a few laps around the lake. The path was quiet this time of morning, with just a few early joggers and dog-walkers out. She slowed her pace, scanning faces, looking for any sign of Marcus.

After a while, she left the park, heading out onto the road and through the nearby neighborhoods. She rode past the coffee shop, carefully averting her eyes, then circled back to the park.

After riding the lake path twice more, Bethany took a break to rest and hydrate. She found an unoccupied bench, pulled out her water and an energy bar and let herself enjoy the view. The bench was facing the lake. She could see people walking the loop from across the water. The sun was nicely warm. She closed her eyes and let herself feel it on her skin.

"Bethany?" a female voice said.

Bethany opened her eyes to see a woman in a tank top and yoga pants jogging in place in front of her.

"It is you. How are you?" She stopped jogging and began stretching her legs on the bench by Bethany. She looked familiar. Something tickled at Bethany's memories.

"Lana?"

"Yeah," Lana grinned. She finished stretching one leg and started on the other. "Didn't you used to live near here? I haven't seen you around. I come through here most mornings."

"I still..." Bethany was caught off guard by the encounter and the memories of the dream came flooding back. She wondered if Lana remembered that moment. It if ever haunted her. She proceeded carefully. "I still live nearby. How are *you*?"

Bethany fully took in the person before her and some of her worry subsided. This Lana was not the nail-biting, cubicle-working Lana she had seen in the dream. There was no way it was the same person. This Lana seemed confident and outgoing.

"I'm good," Lana said. "Better and better all the time, actually."

"Okay," Bethany couldn't help but smile at the optimism, but she was having a hard time reconciling this reality to what she had seen. Maybe the dream wasn't as real as she thought. "That sounds pretty awesome. How do you do that?"

Lana stopped stretching and looked at Bethany seriously.

"You find a goal that lights you up and then become the person who can achieve it." She then grinned again. "At least that's what works for me. I used to have a job that was sucking the life out of me, but I decided I was better than that." She began jogging in place again.

"That's amazing," Bethany said. She found herself a little envious of Lana's self-assurance. "You look like you're doing great."

"Thanks," Lana said. "Sorry to chat and literally run, but I'm on a tight schedule today. Maybe I'll see you around again."

"Sure. Take care," Bethany said as Lana ran off onto the trail. Bethany watched her, lots of questions buzzing in her mind. She knew the dream had shown her the predictable future for Lana. She was sure of it. Somehow Lana had maneuvered her way out of it. And if she could do it, maybe Bethany could, too.

Bethany finished her energy bar, drank some water, then hopped back on her bike. She had a goal and the person who would achieve that goal was a person who didn't stop searching.

Bethany explored side streets she'd never noticed before. She was surprised at the number of people walking about, coming and going, living their lives without the benefit of seeing their futures first. Perhaps her gift wasn't as much of a gift as she thought. These normal people seemed naturally brave. At least, it seemed that way to her.

By early afternoon, Bethany's legs were tired, and she stopped in the park again on her way home. She found another bench to rest on and drank more water. The park was busier, and, instead of watching the lake, she watched the people as she contemplated her next actions.

She couldn't ride her bike endlessly. Her legs were already telling her that wouldn't work. She also didn't want to sit all day in the park with everyone wondering why she was sitting all day in the park. She also didn't want to be recognized as the star-spangled underwear lady. That thought made her survey the area for anyone that might have noticed her.

No one was paying her any attention. They all seemed intent on their own experience in the park. Children played in the grass, joggers darted around walkers on the trail. Dogs pranced happily at the end of their leashes, stopping to sniff and pee while their owners chatted. It was a pleasant tableau of everyday interactions with nature and other people.

Seeing the different shapes of people and movements reminded Bethany that she had brought her sketchbook and tablet. She pulled out the tablet and opened a blank canvas on her screen and began sketching simple lined characters based on what she was seeing.

One lady stretched into downward dog on her yoga mat. Bethany did a quick sketch of the pose. A little girl poked at something with a stick on the edge of the lake. That made it onto the screen as well.

She wasn't sure what she would do with any of these, but the process was fun. She'd relied on wooden mannequins and online pictures for poses the last few years. It got the job done. There was something playful in being here, though, watching people shift in mood and how they stood or walked.

After about an hour or so after starting, Bethany decided to finally call it a day. She was hungrier for more than a snack. She looked over her sketches with a bit of pride. Her career as an illustrator wasn't over yet. And she had no intention of letting it. If she couldn't work things out with Jenna, she would have to learn how to do what she did.

This kind of work felt too good, too right, and she knew she would find a way to keep doing it, even if the thought of that terrified her a little at the moment.

"One thing at a time," Bethany said to herself as she put her tablet away and began heading back home. A story began forming in her mind of that kid-version of herself learning how to overcome fear of the unknown, to embrace mistakes and learn from them.

As she walked her bike down the path towards her house, she realized that even though she hadn't glimpsed Marcus, she didn't feel discouraged. For the first time in a long time, she felt like she was actually living rather than just observing and manipulating life from her safe room.

Chapter Twelve

The sound of the fridge opening and closing startled Bethany as she walked into the house after parking her bike in the garage and going inside.

"Hello?" she said tentatively, as she peeked around the corner into the kitchen.

"It's me," Jenna's said. She was standing by the fridge, drinking a store-bought protein shake. Her tone was unreadable.

Bethany walked in and dropped her backpack on the table.

"Hi," she said, turning to Jenna and giving her full attention.

"I wondered where you were," Jenna said. "I wasn't sure how long I would have to wait."

"There was something I needed to do," Bethany said. "Where's

Rufus?"

"Melody is keeping him," Jenna said. "I felt like we needed to talk without a bunch of distraction."

"Okay," Bethany said. "I'm glad we can talk again."

"Look-"

"I-"

They both began. Jenna put up her hand to silence Bethany. Bethany swallowed and prepared herself to take whatever Jenna was going to say to her. She nodded for Jenna to go on.

"Look, Bethany," Jenna said with a sigh. "I'm not going to make this hard."

That caught Bethany's attention in an ominous way. She opened her mouth to speak.

"Wait," Jenna went on. "I still don't know if I believe you completely, but I believe you enough. It explains a lot. And you have to understand that it sucks to know you've been manipulated."

"I know...," Bethany began.

"There's more." Jenna put her hand up again. "I also don't know what I would have done if I had the same ability." She frowned and seemed to be imagining it. She shrugged. "Maybe I would have been even worse."

"Does that mean you forgive me?" Bethany asked slowly. She

frowned, confused, but relieved, at how quickly Jenna had changed her mind.

"I don't know," Jenna said. "I'm also still sore from the surgery, still coming off pain medication, moving around more than I should, and probably not thinking clearly."

"I haven't been thinking clearly and I don't even have those excuses," Bethany said. "I feel like I'm getting off easier than I should."

"You probably are," Jenna said. "But I was thinking about it last night. My life hasn't been terrible. I don't know how you've nudged me about, but I'm okay with my choices. I'm pretty sure your gift doesn't give you the power to make my choices."

"I hadn't actually thought about it," Bethany said. She leaned on the kitchen counter, thinking through it. "I definitely can't make anyone do anything. But if the possibility is there, I can make it easier and more appealing to go the way I would like it to go."

"That sounds so shady when you say it out loud. You know that, right?" Jenna said. "I only believe you because I can think of several times where I'm two or three steps in on doing something for you before I stop to wonder if I really wanted to do it. How could you do that to someone? Especially a friend. Am I a friend?" Jenna set her shake down and looked at Bethany. "Or just a useful ally?

"You're definitely a friend," Bethany said. She moved over to the table and sat down. "You were the one person who I thought was benefiting as much as me from the choices I made."

Jenna tilted her head, listening.

"I'm really sorry," Bethany went on.

"When was the first time you did it? Do you remember?" Jenna asked. She walked over slowly to the table and eased herself down into a chair.

"Very clearly," Bethany said, thinking of the dream. "Remember when we had to rewrite that book ending for English class and I was happy to write it, but I didn't want to read it out loud?"

"I do remember that," Jenna said. "I thought it was a dumb assignment. But then all I had to do was read it." She looked over at Bethany. "That actually worked out pretty well for me."

Bethany let out a relieved sigh.

"Well, at least I got it right one time," she said.

"Are you saying you wouldn't have thought of that without using your gift?"

"Of course not," Bethany said. "I would have thought you'd be mad at me for trying to get out of doing that part of that project. The vision showed me how to present in a way you'd be okay with the idea."

"Hmmm…," Jenna narrowed her eyes at Bethany for a moment. She pulled out her phone and began typing out a message.

"What are you doing?"

"I'm asking Melody to keep Rufus for tonight so we can talk longer." Jenna looked over at Bethany. "If that is okay with you?"

"Of course!" Bethany said.

"Don't get too excited," Jenna said. "You're probably going to have to help me with making food and carrying stuff. I'll have to sleep on the couch. It will be the easiest for me to get up and down on."

"Okay with me," Bethany smiled. "I'll bring in my sleeping bag and we can have a sleepover in the living room."

"Don't make it weird, Beth," Jenna said, but she was smiling. "By the way, how do I know you won't use your ability on me again? Or even that you're not using it now?"

"For one, it still hasn't been working," Bethany said. "For another, I think part of that is I need to figure out how to navigate these uncomfortable situations on my own."

"Oh, yeah?"

"Yeah," Bethany said. "I think this one, between me and you, is probably the most important to me."

"Because I find you work?" Jenna asked. "And do a lot of the crappy stuff for you?"

"No," Bethany said. "Because we were friends even before I knew I had this gift. And I want to keep that."

Jenna's phone buzzed and she checked it.

"Melody is going to keep Rufus and bring him over in the morning. I was going to grab his piggy, but he'll have to live without it for one night."

"That's rough," Bethany smiled.

"We all have to go through hardship," Jenna said. "At least most of us." She eyed Bethany.

"That's fair," Bethany said. "I seem to be making up for it."

Jenna shook her head.

"I feel like we have a lot of catching up to do, even though I've been in your life all these years."

"And I'm grateful for that," Bethany said. "I really kinda hoped that our partnership was one that worked well for both of us."

"I've given up a lot of jobs for you," Jenna said. "I've given up other clients." Jenna threw up her hands in disbelief. "Like I said before, I was going to move and you convinced me to stay here with you. It's diabolical."

"When you lay it out like that," Bethany said. "Yeah."

"Okay, it's time to get situated on the couch," Jenna said, standing slowly. "We have a lot to talk about."

"I'll help," Bethany said. The cushions were still on the couch from the day before, and Bethany moved them to support Jenna as she sat down.

"You said you tried to tell me when we were younger?" Jenna

finally said.

"I did," Bethany said. "When it first happened in high school. You didn't believe me."

"Well, what about later?" Jenna said. "You only tried once?"

"After that, I didn't see the point," Bethany said.

"Ah. You mean you didn't want to mess up a good thing?"

"Maybe," Bethany said. "The older you get, it seems the more complicated things are. I feel like I've spent a lot of time in my safe room."

"Safe room?"

"That's what I call it," Bethany said.

"I have so many questions," Jenna said. "How does it work? Why do you call it a safe room?"

"Well," Bethany began, "When I shift into the safe room, time stops for me. I call it a safe room, because I feel like nothing can touch me there. My consciousness is outside the physical realm. The options for potential futures are displayed on a wall of the room, and I check them to see which one I want to happen. Then I do whatever I have to do."

"So, you just go through the motions?" Jenna asked.

"It feels that way more and more," Bethany said. She could feel her body releasing tension as they spoke. "Geez. It feels really good to talk about this. I feel like I've been going crazy lately trying to make everything work. I feel exhausted over it."

"Now that I know, you know we're going to have to discuss using your ability to get more clients," Jenna laughed. It was a nice sound.

"I don't know." Bethany couldn't help a small whine. The conversation was going well. If Jenna could be this open, she could do the same. "Maybe."

Jenna laughed again.

"I'm kidding, Beth," she said. "It sounds like you've been using your ability to protect yourself, and I can understand that. If I didn't have to deal with some of the stuff I have had to deal with … but I'm curious. What happened that made it stop working?"

Bethany rolled her eyes.

"I'm kinda embarrassed about it."

"No way. What happened?"

"Okay," Bethany said. "Don't laugh, but I met my soulmate or whatever term you want to call it."

"Are you serious? It wasn't Caleb?"

"No," Bethany said with a friendly glare.

"I never understood why you two divorced. Surely you could have worked it…" Jenna stopped as she realized. "Did you see something with him?"

Bethany answered with silence. She didn't want to talk about it. She wasn't ready for that. Not even with Jenna.

"Okay," Jenna said. "One thing at a time. So you met your soulmate." She smirked at the term. "Who is he? Are you going out?"

"No," Bethany frowned. "I don't even know how to find him. I've run into him twice and both times everything went off the rails. All I know is that his name is Marcus."

"Marcus," Jenna said. "So he lives around here?"

"I ran into him for the first time at the Village Pantry and then in the park."

"Our park?" Jenna exclaimed. "And all you got was his first name?"

"I don't even know how to explain," Bethany said, rubbing her forehead. "Like I said, neither time was the best ever circumstances."

"But you know he is … the one," Jenna said dramatically.

"My gift auto-started when I first saw him and I caught glimpses of our life together, a perfect marriage of individuality and trust."

"Well," Jenna said, dryly. "Sounds sexy."

"That's there, too," Bethany said with a tight smile. "No worries. And I will not be explaining how I know that."

"Okay," Jenna said with a look that indicated they would circle back around to that. "Maybe we should try to figure out why things aren't working the way they should."

"I kinda know," Bethany said. "I've had these strange dreams lately. It's like meeting Marcus triggered all this. And because I have been short-cutting parts of my life and, apparently, not learning my lessons, I'm playing catch-up. I'm not sure it's worth it." Bethany shook her head. "Actually, I do think it's worth it, which is why I'm even having this conversation."

"What kinds of lessons did you short-cut?" Jenna said. "I don't get it."

"Like I said before, a lot of times I'm acting my way through situations," Bethany said. "It seems that to learn the lesson, I have to process the emotions that come with them. I think some of the crazy stuff that has been happening lately has to do with balancing that out."

"Crazy stuff?"

Bethany looked pointedly over at Jenna.

"You haven't heard about the park incident?"

"Uh ... no," Jenna said.

"I suppose that's good," Bethany said. She wasn't sure she wanted to get into it. "Let's just say I've been going through some embarrassing moments and scary situations—like Meredith—and having to get through them."

"That's just growing up," Jenna said.

Goddess Game

"And where I've been cheating," Bethany shrugged.

"You can't worry about what people think, Beth. Life is random sometimes," Jenna said. "I suppose the rest of us have more practice with that."

"It's eye-opening," Bethany said. "And it feels like I'm just tumbling in and out of situations I would rather avoid."

"I can see how that would suck," Jenna said. "Are you sure you're not using your gift? I'm starting to feel sorry for you."

"I'm not," Bethany said. She tried it just to see what would happen, and it suddenly worked and she could how she could use this conversation to make everything right with Jenna.

All she had to do was…

Bethany left the safe room before she could see the actions she needed to take and the words she needed to say. She was enjoying being real with Jenna. She didn't dare mess it up. "I'm really not."

Chapter Thirteen

Bethany was dreaming again.

It felt like another life. She stood in the two-bedroom apartment that she and Caleb had lived in for most of their marriage. The details were crystal clear - the slightly crooked blinds that never quite hung right, the light gray walls Caleb had insisted would make the space feel bigger, a stack of art supplies cluttering the top of a small desk in the corner of the living room. Every inch held memories, some sweet, some bitter.

When Bethany's mom had died, Caleb had wanted her to sell the house and then buy one that would be new for them and more their style. But her mom's house was her style. And it felt like she had been compromising to all his likings for years. The house had become a symbol of their fundamental disconnect—Caleb wanting change while Bethany clung to the familiar, the safe.

This was when the anger began to build up and staying married didn't seem worth the trouble. It was starting to show up in arguments and small confrontations that seemed insignificant, but she saw how it would end. She had seen it for years. She even knew before they were married.

Her relationship with Caleb was the one time she fought against the visions she saw. She had tried so many different things to change it. Caleb had been safe, reliable, kind. She'd thought she could change the future if she tried hard enough.

Each morning, she'd slip into her safe room, searching for the perfect words, the right actions to keep them together. But the visions always eventually showed a path of unhappiness and resentment. Her efforts each day kept Caleb from seeing it as clearly as she did. But she knew he must have felt it.

As time went on, she became more and more tired. She knew they would have to get a divorce but couldn't bring herself to do it. She felt guilty. There were women who dealt with much worse than she did. Unlike her, though, they didn't see the future and years lost to bitterness.

The visions had become increasingly dark - showing her how her continued attempts to force their relationship would poison what good remained between them. She saw Caleb's dreams withering, saw her own creativity stagnating. None of the outcomes of her vision led to a life that worked for both of them being together.

She was using her gift with him multiple times a day, and it wasn't getting better. They wanted different things out of life. It didn't make either of them bad, but they were pulling at each other, neither wanting to budge from the path that felt most natural for them to follow.

Finally, Bethany could see no other option. She had to give Caleb up for both of their sakes. She could see that he would have a better life if they were divorced. It was probably the only time she used her gift in a way where she wasn't thinking of herself at all.

As she was remembering all of this, Caleb came through the front door of the apartment with a few bags of groceries and began putting them away. She watched him move around the kitchen with familiar efficiency, remembering how they'd once danced around each other in this space, young and in love and believing that would be enough.

This was the day, the day she told him.

Bethany felt like a passenger in the dream. She watched herself walk over to Caleb, knowing what was coming and powerless to change it.

"I've been thinking," Bethany began. For a moment, she didn't think she would be able to say it, but then she thought of him and how she was holding him back from a better life. She blurted out the words, "It would be best for the both of us if we got a divorce."

Surprisingly, Caleb nodded, as if he suspected this was coming.

Or perhaps he had wanted it and was afraid to say it. Maybe he'd felt the same inevitable pull apart that she had, just without the supernatural confirmation.

She couldn't see the visions in the dream, but she knew she was using her safe room with each response. She didn't want to risk any further stress or anger than what she had already internalized. Even in ending things, she was trying to control the outcome, to make it as painless as possible.

They were separated for a year. She was successful in avoiding him, allowing him to experience his life without her interfering. After the year, they went before a judge and it was done. It was strange to close the door on such a long period in their life.

When they had encountered each other a few months after the divorce was final, it felt like bumping into an old friend. Caleb hadn't seemed to harbor any hard feelings and was thriving, already making plans for the bookstore. Bethany felt good about that part.

"So many lessons tied up in that memory," Fiona said softly from behind Bethany. "So many more to learn."

Bethany felt tears streaming down her cheeks.

"I never wanted to hurt him," she said. The truth of it ached in her chest. She had tried so hard to prevent pain that she'd caused it, anyway.

"He seems to be fine," Fiona said. "Are you?"

Bethany let herself crumpled to the ground. She had never allowed herself to grieve the loss of her first love. She had all those years tied up in trying to make the marriage work when she knew all along that it never would. The safety she'd sought had become a cage, trapping them both in a half-life of compromise.

"It's okay," Fiona said. "Take your time." *She sat beside Bethany and put her arm around her.* "Even when you lose, there is something to learn. Nothing is wasted. This is important."

As Bethany spent several long moments in the dream sobbing. It felt good to let it out. When she was done, Fiona lifted her face to meet her eyes.

"I have done what I can to help you. It is up to you now. These dreams have been calibrations, but you have to continue the work in the waking world."

Fiona wiped the tears from Bethany's cheeks with part of her dress.

"It's so overwhelming," *Bethany whispered.* "I don't know how to make it all work."

"Seek out your fears and get ahead of the game," *Fiona said matter-of-factly.* "It's the only way you will bring to you what you want. Anything else you experience in life is you being caught up in the ebb and flow of people bumping up against each other. Do you want to be in control or controlled?"

Fiona stood, regal and radiant as ever. She looked down on Bethany with compassion, and yet there was a defiant challenge in her eyes.

"Your move," she said.

She watched as Bethany straightened herself up into a sitting position. Fiona nodded and then disappeared.

Bethany jerked further into awareness as she found herself all alone and back in the cage.

This time, though, felt different. The scene was the same. The cliff was overhead. The wave was coming. However, Bethany wasn't the same.

Bethany considered what Fiona said. She wanted to be in control - real control, not the illusion of it she'd had with her gift. She imagined herself out of the cage and standing on the cliff, facing the wave. The scene shifted, and she was there. The wave was rolling forward, as gigantic and terrifying as ever.

Bethany suddenly felt like she understood what was happening. She held her ground despite her growing trepidation, and, when the wave was close enough to break over her, she dove forward, headfirst, piercing through the wall of water about to obliterate everything in its wake.

Once inside the wave, Bethany felt a sense of relief and safety. She found she could swim through the water easily and to the surface, away from its destructive power. As she bobbed in what just appeared to be a normal ocean, she wondered what she should do next.

It seemed completely up to her.

Chapter Fourteen

Bethany's phone was ringing. It was mid-morning and she had completed most of her routine bookkeeping. She grinned like a kid finishing the last school assignment before summer break. That afternoon, she would work on one of her personal illustration projects.

As she looked over at her phone, she saw the caller was Caleb and hesitated. She wasn't sure she wanted to answer. The memories in the dream were still felt fresh. Bethany was worried that in her guilt she might burst out crying, and he wouldn't even understand what was going on.

Breathe, she told herself. *And think through it.*

That helped her gain a little presence of mind. If she thought about things as they were now, essentially nothing had changed. They were still friends. And, after her talk with Jenna, she realized that for her and Caleb to have lasted for as long as they did, there was enough of something there for him or she wouldn't have been able to make it work.

She thought about that for a moment. What if, in the struggles of their relationship, he was learning and refining the resilience he needed to make his current life goals work? Fiona said she had cheated herself. And, while her manipulations seemed to influence others, they were all in control of their own lives in the same way she was.

She answered the call.

"Hey, what's up?"

"Hey, I was hoping you could come by the bookstore this afternoon," Caleb said.

"You want me to show my face in the bookstore this soon?" Bethany asked. She was only slightly joking.

Caleb laughed.

"I forgot about that," he said.

"I bet no one else has," Bethany said. "I never will."

"It was that good, huh?"

"Fun-ny," Bethany said, playfully. She suddenly appreciated the fact that they could still be friends. That had really been the most important part of their relationship all along. "What's going on?"

"Nothing urgent," Caleb said. "I have an idea and I would like your input ... and your help, if you are willing."

"That's pretty vague," Bethany said. "But you've caught me in my 'open to new things' phase."

"That sounds interesting," he said. "I'll take what advantage I can. And you sort of owe me one."

"I guess I do," Bethany said. "You just need me? Do I need to bring anything?"

"Just yourself. It will make sense when you get here. When would be a good time for you?"

"Does it have to be this afternoon? I could come by now," Bethany offered. She was almost done with her work, anyway.

"Great, even better," Caleb said. "I'll be waiting for you."

Bethany decided to lean into whatever was coming. She biked over to the bookstore and found Caleb inside, waiting for her.

"Come check this out," he said, leading her to the back corner of the bookstore where the children's books were located.

Bethany right away noticed several books with her "illustrated by Bethany Hart" on them.

"Nice selection," she smiled.

Goddess Game

"Yep," Caleb nodded. "What would be even nicer is if I knew an illustrator that could create a unique mural for this area." He pointed out the walls around the children's books, which were colorful, but not very imaginative. The children's area had a small table and bean bags for kids to sit and read.

"That's what you brought me down here for?" Bethany asked.

"It's harder to say no if you have to look me in the face," Caleb said with a smile. Bethany didn't smile back at first. Her guilt came floating up. That was hers to work out, though. She managed an interested smile as she looked the area over. There was possibility, but she had only painted a couple murals for school, never by herself.

"I don't know, Caleb," she said. "I haven't done anything that big before."

"It's not as hard as you think," Caleb said. "I saw someone do something like this by drawing it small scale and then using a projector to project it on the wall. After the drawing, it's just a matter of painting."

"Really?" Bethany said. "Sounds like cheating."

"I'd say it is using a tool creatively," Caleb said. "Once you have everything lined up, you can take your time on the details. You get to plan it out before you take that next step and make changes in the small version before you even start the work. It actually seems really smart to me."

"Okay, okay," Bethany said. "Do you have anything particular in mind? A theme?"

"Yeah," Caleb said, scratching at the stubble of a beard starting to grow out. "No. I was hoping you could help with that as well. Something that feels inspiring and visionary yet doesn't take away from reading."

"That's all?" Bethany laughed. She considered the space and her experience drawing for kids. "How about we leave it at maybe?" she said. "I need to think about it. But you are right. I do you we you one for rescuing me."

Caleb nodded.

"Seriously," he said. "Carrying you to my office was no joke."

"Are you implying that I weigh a lot?" Bethany asked, her eyebrow raised.

"Of course not," Caleb said quickly. "Surely I'm just older and my back isn't what it used to be."

"Right," Bethany smiled.

Caleb turned serious.

"You seem better now. Everything working itself out?"

"I think so," Bethany said. "I think so."

"Good," he said.

"So, was that it?" Bethany asked.

"That's it," Caleb said. "I appreciate you coming over and

considering it," he said. "Just let me know how much you want to charge. I'll buy the paint and whatever you need. I already have a projector."

"Okay," Bethany said. She looked at the walls again, seeing how she could create a design emerging out of the bookshelves. It could be fun.

She took a picture of the area with her phone and began walking towards the door. As she was leaving, Caleb hurried over. "Don't forget game night at my house tonight. 7 PM."

"Maybe," Bethany said.

"I'm still cashing in on that 'open to new things' phase."

Bethany smiled and nodded. He had her there.

"Okay," she said and left before she got roped into anything else.

Back home, Bethany met a frantic Jenna at the door.

"Meredith called," Jenna said. Rufus was back home and hovering around her protectively.

"Uh-oh," Bethany said. All the good feelings of the day became nervous butterflies. "What did she say?"

"She wants you to meet her again. At her house. In an hour."

"Did she say anything else?" Bethany tensed at the thought of her recapping what had happened that day in the coffee shop.

"No," Jenna said. "Did you hear what I said, though? We have another shot at the job."

"What? I don't know," Bethany said. It felt like everything was building up to overwhelm her again.

"Seriously, Beth," Jenna said. "Didn't we just talk about facing fears and all?"

Bethany looked at Jenna, her initial fear replaced with slight indignation.

"Are you trying to manipulate me now?"

"All's fair," Jenna smiled mischievously. "Really, though, it is a good opportunity. There's no reason you shouldn't get this job and the rewards that come from being attached to a well-known project."

Bethany remembered that her gift had worked last night when she tried it. Perhaps she could use it this go round with Meredith? She couldn't bring herself to think about it. What if she had a repeat performance of what had happened at the coffee shop? Caleb wouldn't be there to help her escape. If she was going to do it, she was going to have to do it with no outside or inside help.

Bethany could feel her fear bubbling up and then, behind that, she remembered the wave in the dream. She took a deep breath. "Give me the address."

"I'll text it to you," Jenna said, her surprise evident in her tone. "Good luck."

Bethany took a few minutes to change. She could at least look a bit more professional before round two with Meredith. She didn't know how she was going to explain what had happened at their last meeting.

Please, please, please don't ask me that, Bethany thought.

Bethany drove over to the address Jenna gave her and parked on the street outside a formidable brick house. It fit Meredith's personality. Bethany rang the bell and Meredith opened the door, looking as stern as ever.

"There you are," she said, gesturing Bethany inside. "This way."

She led Bethany to an office with colorful illustration prints all over the walls. It didn't fit in with Bethany's impression of Meredith at all, but, judging from the computer and papers and a half-empty cup of coffee, this was the place Meredith managed her work.

"We didn't get to talk much last time," Meredith began. She raised her eyebrows at Bethany. "You are feeling better now?"

Bethany considered joking that she was feeling better at that time, but refrained. The situation was so ridiculous to her now that she almost burst out laughing. If only Meredith knew.

"Thank you for asking," Bethany said. "I apologize for making a scene."

"Well," Meredith said. "You seemed quite nervous that day. But you appear more composed today."

"Yes," Bethany said. "I have been doing some soul searching of late. I realized that I have been avoiding a lot, that I should have been embracing or letting go." That came out almost too casually, but Bethany was feeling more comfortable being honest about things. If this was going to work, it would work because Bethany was the right fit. "That's probably more than you wanted to know. In any case, I'm here to talk about your project if you're ready to do that."

Meredith leaned back in her chair, assessing Bethany. She then leaned forward and gestured to a bookcase full of various-sized and various-colored notebooks.

"Do you see all those notebooks?"

"Yes," Bethany said.

"I've been writing stories for children since I was sixteen. That's why I'm able to produce them so quickly. I get one illustrated, then move on to the next one. I didn't even start publishing them until I was in my fifties. Even then, I didn't know they would do well. I was motivated, though, and I still am. It gives me a purpose in my life."

Bethany nodded at this unexpected divulgence.

"I told you I wanted to know about you," Meredith said. "I thought you should know a little about me as well."

"Thank you," Bethany said, but she was confused. She wasn't sure where to go from there.

"You see," Meredith went on. "That's why I like to use mostly unknown talent for my illustrations. I don't want others to wait as long as I did to share themselves with the world." Her mouth twitched briefly into a knowing smile. "It's not fair to the world."

Bethany listened, dumbfounded. She thought of her own work, collecting in her portfolio bag. Before she could form a response, Meredith went on.

"I'll send Jenna the details," she said in her usual authoritative manner. "That's all. You can go."

"What?" Bethany said. "That's it?"

"That's all it needs to be," Meredith said. "What else do you want?"

"You had me come all the way out here for less than ten minutes?"

"You could have not come and not gotten the job." Meredith shrugged. "I told you I like to see who a person is in person. I already knew I liked your work. You seem to be a solid individual." She smiled for a moment, and then it slipped away into sternness again. "You can see yourself out?"

"Sure," Bethany said. She turned back as she left Meredith's office. "Thanks."

Meredith didn't even look up, just waved her away.

Bethany drove home in a daze.

"I got the email. You did it!" Jenna said from the couch as Bethany walked through the door. She had her phone email open and showed Bethany that they had the job offer from Meredith. "Did your ability come back?"

"I didn't dare try it," Bethany said, waving away the questioning look that got her from Jenna. "The meeting wasn't what I expected, but I guess ... we roll with it?"

"Yes, we do," Jenna said. Rufus was on the couch next to her and she gave him some scratches under his chin, then turned to Bethany. "And I've been thinking. We actually have had a pretty good partnership all these years. I'm willing to stick it out for now if you are. Let's just be honest with each other and work through things on equal terms."

"I can live with that," Bethany smiled.

"Great," Jenna said. "I'm still recuperating. Up for a movie night tonight?"

"Would you be okay if I passed on that?" Bethany asked. "Caleb has a game night tonight that he invited me to."

"You've been spending a lot of time with him. Mysterious Marcus might get jealous." Jenna smirked.

"I have to find him first." Bethany rolled her eyes. "I owe Caleb for helping me out. Nothing more."

"All right, all right," Jenna said. "Could you at least set me up with some snacks? And give me the remote?"

"Are you sure you're okay by yourself?" Bethany asked as she watched Jenna adjust herself on the couch. It suddenly didn't feel right to leave her. "I can go to the game night another Friday."

"Go," Jenna said. "I wouldn't mind having a night to myself." She looked over at Rufus. "Well, with my buddy, I mean."

Bethany almost decided not to go. She thought of the people there that she might now know. She would have to make small talk. Still, she had told Caleb she would go. And Jenna looked like she needed a night of rest. Jenna seemed fine with the idea and was already scrolling through movies.

"Text me if you need anything?" Bethany suggested.

"Sure," Jenna answered without looking away from the TV.

Bethany hurried out the door before she thought of any other reasons not to go.

Chapter Fifteen

The fifteen-minute drive to Caleb's house was more of an internal struggle than Bethany anticipated. Several times she halfway convinced herself that Jenna had passed out and hit her head or somehow tore a stitch open or some random emergency that required Bethany to turn around and go home. But the phone never buzzed. Maybe Jenna really was okay on her own.

Bethany slowed down as her mind did its best to manufacture an excuse to not go. Fortunately, the road to Caleb's had little traffic at this hour. Two cars passed her though, their drivers probably wondering why she was barely maintaining twenty-five miles per hour in a thirty-five zone. She picked up to a normal speed, recommitted to showing up.

Of course, then she wondered if showing up was really a big deal. She likely would just sit around in awkward silence. She imagined no one would want to talk to her or they might think she was boring or weird—things she'd often worried about since she was a teenager. Bethany reminded herself that she was thirty-eight and a capable adult - at least on most days. She had navigated plenty of social situations, although, admittedly, she'd had some help with that.

She also reasoned that, in the worst-case scenario, she could always leave. She didn't even have to make a dramatic exit - she could simply talk to Caleb, explain how she was feeling, and go home. Maybe try again another time. That thought was reassuring, like having an escape route planned.

Deciding to make the best of the drive, Bethany consciously tried to enjoy the journey. She rarely drove long distances, preferring her bike or walking, and it was actually nice to see unique architecture and scenery than what she usually encountered.

Since there were no longer any cars behind her, she slowed down again and really looked at the homes and landscaping. Even though it was getting close to 7 PM, it was still fairly light out. The houses in this section of town were older and had the kind of architectural details you didn't see in newer developments - ornate trim work, stained glass windows, wrap-around porches that spoke of lazy Sunday afternoons.

Caleb had stayed in a couple of different apartments after they divorced, but by the time he moved into his house, they were talking again as friends and she had helped him move in. She realized she hadn't paid much attention to how interesting the homes were. She had mainly wanted to help and then get home as soon as possible.

Now that she was looking at the neighborhood, she thought she might ask Caleb if she could sit on his porch sometime, sketching, and doing a study of the different styles of houses. It never hurt to expand her repertoire for future illustrations. She could already imagine how some of these architectural details might translate into the backgrounds for children's books.

A flash of movement in her peripheral vision caused her to hit the brakes just as a couple of deer bounded across the road, their white tails flashing in the evening light. Her heart hammered in her chest as she watched them disappear into someone's yard. If she hadn't been paying attention, she not only wouldn't have made it to game night, she could have easily totaled her car. She sat there for a moment, hands shaking somewhat as she took several deep breaths.

She drove more tentatively after that, even more actively aware of her surroundings. The tension in her shoulders eased as she saw Caleb's house up ahead, only to return full force at the sight of his full driveway and cars parked all along the road. The reality of how many people must be inside struck her like a physical force.

She had known in advance that she would likely be parking on the road, but she wasn't expecting quite so many vehicles. How many people were at this game night? She gritted her teeth and began looking for a spot, determined not to let this be the thing

Goddess Game

that sent her running home. There was one spot close by that she'd have to parallel park in, or she could drive down further and see if there was parking on another block.

Where's the growth?, she thought to herself. She wasn't used to thinking this way yet, but she understood what was at stake. While she might not be perfect at it for a while, she would keep pressing where it seemed obvious to do so. After a few careful corrections, she backed into the spot. Thank goodness for having a small car.

She locked up and made her way across the street, up the driveway, and to the walkway that led up to the porch. The front of the house glowed warmly, and she could hear muffled laughter from inside. She hesitated at the base of the steps, that familiar urge to flee rising again. She could still get away before anyone saw her.

"You here for the game night?" a friendly female voice called from behind her. Bethany turned to see two women coming up the driveway, both carrying bags that clinked with the telltale sound of bottles.

"Nice. A new victim…" the other lady said with a playful grin.

"Ignore her," the first woman said, rolling her eyes good-naturedly. "She's overly competitive. I'm Rachel. This is my sister Samantha."

"Hi," Bethany said, suddenly grateful for their appearance. "Caleb didn't tell me to bring anything." She gestured at their bags, feeling empty-handed.

"We always bring our own stuff. You're welcome to share," Rachel offered warmly.

"Thanks," Bethany said, already feeling more at ease. These women seemed nice enough, and their casual manner helped dissolve some of her anxiety.

"Let's head in," Rachel said. "See who all showed up tonight."

"Lead the way," Bethany said, falling in behind Rachel and Samantha. Something about having these two as a buffer made crossing the threshold feel less daunting.

It was strange seeing Caleb's house after so long. The last time she had been inside, he was still living out of boxes and it had been a bit of a wreck. Now, everything was organized, the space transformed into a warm and inviting home.

Rachel and Samantha entered as if they were family, reminding Bethany that the game night had been going on for a while. These people had their own rhythms and relationships, and she was stepping into an established dynamic.

The living room had several small tables set up with sets of four people already seated. Caleb was at the dining table, which had room for six people to sit. He got up immediately when he saw Bethany and came over to greet her, his familiar presence instantly comforting.

"I'm glad you came. The gang's all here so we can get started. I know you don't want to be a spectacle, so I'll just introduce you to the folks at my table for now." He turned to the table and gestured to the people sitting there. Four people were already seated, and that increased to six after Rachel and Samantha joined them. "This is Bethany. I hope she'll come back so you all behave." He began introducing each person around the table.

Bethany waved at each one and then froze. Marcus leaned forward from beside an older woman as he was introduced. She could tell by the mischievous twinkle in his eyes that he recognized her as well. Her heart skipped a beat.

"Hi, everyone," Bethany said, her voice steadier than she felt. "I probably won't remember all the names right away, but it's nice to meet you."

"It looks like we have an even number now," Caleb said. "It will be a bit of stretch with three pairs, but is everyone up for a game of Canasta?"

A cheer went up from the table.

"Let's pair up, then," Caleb said. He turned to Bethany as she tugged at his shirt.

"I've never played that game," Bethany whispered.

"You can be my partner," Caleb said. "You'll be fine."

Caleb sat down and when Bethany went to sit beside him, he indicated the chair across from him.

"Partners sit across from one another," he said.

"Oh," Bethany said, and moved around to the table to her seat. The others shifted as well to be across from their partners and within a few seconds, Marcus was seated on her left. The Universe, it seemed, had a sense of humor.

"Hi, again," he said softly. "So, you and Caleb…?"

"Not exactly. He's actually my ex."

"You dated?"

"We were married," Bethany clarified, watching his reaction carefully.

"Interesting," Marcus said, his expression thoughtful. "And you still hang out?"

"Long story," Bethany said with a slight smile. "We didn't work as married. We work as friends."

"Ah," Marcus nodded, seeming to accept this.

A huge deck of cards was being split apart amongst each person. The familiar motions of card-dealing provided a welcome distraction from the electricity she felt sitting next to Marcus.

"Do you know Caleb from the bookstore?" Bethany asked, trying to keep her voice casual.

"No. My mom just moved in next door," he said, point to the older woman across the table from him. "I was just in town helping her get settled. I'm going back home in the morning."

"Oh," Bethany said, her heart sinking slightly at this news. "Hi," she waved at his mom, mind racing with questions she wasn't sure how to ask without seeming too eager. She thought about trying out her gift to see if it worked, but didn't bother. It was actually a little fun not knowing and seeing how things played out naturally. "So you're here under duress?"

Marcus laughed, the sound warming something inside her. "A little. But I don't mind. I'm glad she has a good neighbor and now a group of people she can hang out with," he said.

"Yeah, Caleb is a good person to know," Bethany agreed.

"So, it seems a little weird to not comment on our last interaction," he said as he took his share of the cards. Bethany felt herself reddening at the memory. "I had a similar experience when I was in high school," he continued. "I think I changed my name and moved away. You seem to be faring well."

Bethany sighed, but found herself smiling. "What else can I do?" she said. "What is done is done. I can't undo it at this point."

"True," Marcus said, his eyes crinkling at the corners. Bethany took her share of the cards.

"Shuffle, and then make two stacks of thirteen cards," Caleb said to Bethany when she looked confused. She nodded and began shuffling. She wasn't sure how long she should go, but started counting out her decks as the others did.

"You'll give one stack to the person on your left and one to the person on your right," Caleb said.

She handed Marcus a stack. Samantha was on her right and she passed a stack over to her. Samantha gave her one right back.

Bethany turned to Marcus, waiting on the stack from him. He was holding it in his hands and saying, "May it be filled with red threes, all the red threes."

Caleb laughed and looked at Bethany. "Red threes are the worst cards."

Bethany took the cards from Marcus. "Did you just hate on my cards?"

"Yes," he said, that mischievous sparkle dancing in his eyes again.

"Well, then," Bethany said, relaxing into the playful moment. This felt comfortable, natural. This was a start. She didn't even need to tap into her gift to realize it. She was even thinking back to what Fiona had said about her not tapping into her full power. That could be something worth exploring. But on another day.

Marcus might leave tomorrow, but now she knew he would likely be back. Everyone visits their mother, right? This was her opportunity to make the connection she needed to make.

Bethany put one stack of cards down like everyone else and began placing the rest of her cards in the cardholder. There were so many. She had no idea what was good, what was bad, or what the goal was. But she knew she wanted to play well, even if she didn't win today.

She looked at Caleb and smiled, feeling a warmth in the moment that had nothing to do with her cards. "What are the rules to this game, anyway?"

Epilogue

Fiona floated in the light and darkness of everything. Her presence and shape were the only form in this space between dimensions. She glowed with an inner radiance that pulsed in harmony with the cosmic frequencies around her. Her consciousness, expanded beyond normal human comprehension, easily spanned across time and space, allowing her to observe multiple realities simultaneously.

She smiled, her eyes closed, but her awareness was perfectly attuned to the threads of probability flowing around her. She was particularly focused on one thread - Bethany's current timeline. Fiona watched with satisfaction as Bethany navigated her conversation with Jenna, saw the playfulness entering her demeanor, followed the thread forward to her arrival at Caleb's house and the promising interaction with Marcus.

The pieces were falling into place, just as they had in her own past, countless lifetimes ago. That memory - though "memory" was an inadequate word for the multidimensional awareness she now possessed - was particularly precious to her.

Another form appeared beside Fiona. A masculine presence materialized, his energy signature both familiar and beloved. Fiona opened her eyes to acknowledge him, though in this elevated state of being, the boundaries that separated them were so thin as to be nearly nonexistent. The light that emanated from them both mingled together intimately, creating patterns of sacred geometry in the space between.

"I thought I would find you here," the man said or thought - at this level of ascension, communication transcended ordinary speech. "You often come to this time and place."

Fiona smiled, her radiance brightening with affection and recognition.

"This moment is special to you," he said. It wasn't a question - such things were simply known.

"Yes," Fiona said.

"Is there something particular about this time?" he asked, though he likely already knew the answer. In their realm, questions were asked not for information but for the joy of shared understanding.

Fiona considered it. She had existed for so long as to be an eternity, her consciousness expanding through dimensions beyond human understanding. Part of advancing to this level of being was the ability to review previous lives and, once reaching this most advanced state, to offer guidance to earlier versions of oneself when necessary. She had done so many times across many timelines. But this life as Bethany, this specific moment in spacetime, felt more special.

"In all of my timelessness," she said, her voice resonating in multiple harmonics, "this lifetime, that period of time was the biggest turn, the moment I truly stepped into an understanding of my power."

The man nodded, his own light pulsing in empathy with her emotions.

"It shines brighter for me than any of my lifetimes—even the ones after where I was so much more capable and powerful," she continued. "This was when I first understood that true power comes not from controlling outcomes, but from having the courage to face uncertainty with an open heart."

Fiona and the man grew silent, their outer glow becoming brighter with their combined joy in the expression of the moment. Their energies created more complex patterns in the cosmic void, telling stories of countless shared lifetimes and lessons learned together.

"Thank you for sharing with me," the man said. "I will leave you to it as I become oneness."

Fiona reached for and took his hand as he began to dissolve. He lingered for a moment and they looked into each other's eyes, sharing millennia of understanding in a single glance, and then he was gone, his energy merging back into the universal consciousness.

Fiona placed her hands together as if in prayer. Her form shifted and her features changed. She now appeared as Bethany, but not the uncertain, fear-driven Bethany of the current timeline. This was Bethany as she would become - powerful, radiant, fully awakened to her true nature. This was Bethany after countless lifetimes of growth, after mastering not just the ability to see possible futures, but the wisdom to know when to let go and simply experience life as it unfolded.

"So, we win," she whispered, her voice carrying the weight of ages and the lightness of perfect understanding.

She began to glow brighter and brighter until her energy spread out around her and she dissipated to become one with all in the universe.

About Sheila Lee Brown

Sheila Lee Brown is a writer, artist, and generally very curious person. She spent her childhood playing outdoors in the woods surrounding her home and making up stories with her three siblings.

Sheila lives with her husband and their dog and enjoys writing, reading, drawing silly cartoons, and always learning and growing.

You can find out more about her upcoming projects at:

www.tz-books.com

Note from the Author

Thanks for reading *Goddess Game*. As a creative introvert, writing this book and following Bethany on her journey (really the start of a longer journey) reminded me of the times that I've held myself back because the world sometimes seems too unknowable and risky.

It also reminded me that there is no losing in life—you either actually accomplish what you want or you learn from it. In either case, you've got to take action to figure that part out. I find it to be a valuable lesson.

If you enjoyed reading this book, would you please take a moment to leave me a review at your favorite retailer?

Thanks, and best wishes!

Sheila Lee Brown

Made in United States
Orlando, FL
16 March 2025